The Day Before

The Day
Before

LISA SCHROEDER

Simon Pulse
New York   London   Toronto   Sydney

This book is a work of fiction. Any references to historical events, real people, or real locales are used fictitiously. Other names, characters, places, and incidents are the product of the author's imagination, and any resemblance to actual events or locales or persons, living or dead, is entirely coincidental.

SIMON PULSE
An imprint of Simon & Schuster Children's Publishing Division
1230 Avenue of the Americas, New York, NY 10020
First Simon Pulse hardcover edition June 2011
Copyright © 2011 by Lisa Schroeder
All rights reserved, including the right of reproduction in whole or in part in any form.
SIMON PULSE and colophon are registered trademarks of Simon & Schuster, Inc.
For information about special discounts for bulk purchases, please contact Simon & Schuster Special Sales at 1-866-506-1949 or business@simonandschuster.com.
The Simon & Schuster Speakers Bureau can bring authors to your live event. For more information or to book an event contact the Simon & Schuster Speakers Bureau at 1-866-248-3049 or visit our website at www.simonspeakers.com.
Designed by Mike Rosamilia
The text of this book was set in Adobe Garamond.
Manufactured in the United States of America
2 4 6 8 10 9 7 5 3 1
Library of Congress Cataloging-in-Publication Data
Schroeder, Lisa.
The day before / Lisa Schroeder. — 1st Simon Pulse hardcover ed.
p. cm.
Summary: Sixteen-year-old Amber, hoping to spend one perfect day alone at the beach before her world is turned upside down, meets and feels a strong connection to Cade, who is looking for his own escape, for a very different reason.
ISBN 978-1-4424-1743-4
[1. Novels in verse. 2. Interpersonal relations—Fiction. 3. Beaches—Fiction. 4. Family life—Oregon—Fiction. 5. Oregon—Fiction.]
I. Title.
PZ7.5.S37Day 2011
[Fic]—dc22
2010034567
ISBN 978-1-4424-1745-8 (eBook)

This one is for all of you
who feel the fear and do it anyway,
in writing and in life.
You inspire me!

The Day Before

Acknowledgments

Annette Pollert, thank you so much for your enthusiasm and all of your work to make this book the best it could be. On every page you pushed me—kindly and gently—but you pushed, and for that I'm incredibly grateful.

Sara Crowe, I cannot express how much I appreciate your rock solid support and belief in me. A million times, thank you.

Cindy Hanson of the Oregon Coast Aquarium, thank you for your help with my research. Any errors in regards to your fantastic facility are mine, and mine alone.

Bryan Bliss, thanks for asking around and helping me check very important facts. It's true—you're awesome.

Finally, I want to thank *all* of my fans who lift me up with kind words and deeds. People like Maddie, Alex, Kathleen, Sara, Jack, Alyson, Candace, Avonlea, Teresa, Hailee, Skyanne, Anna, Maryanne, Elizabeth, Jessica, Katie, James, Emma, Jasmine, Kristen, Lauren, Delaney, Savannah, and many other wonderful people. Your support means the world to me, really and truly.

a different kind of day

Some mornings,
it's hard to get
out of bed.

Sleep lures you
like a stranger
with a piece of candy.

Follow me.
It will be okay.
I promise.

You know better,
but still you follow,
because you really do
love candy.

When you finally
open your eyes,
late for everything
and your whole day
screwed,
you curse that bastard,
Mr. Sandman.

It's happened to me
a hundred times.
But not today.

Today was different.

Anticipation is the best
alarm there is, and it shook
me awake before
my phone even had
the chance.

As I move around my room
with my iPod on and earbuds in,
my girl P!nk sings strong,
and I feel like I have
superpowers.

The power to
let myself go,
let myself be,
let myself live
the next
twenty-four hours
in a way
I have never lived
before.

ready, set, go

In the bathroom
I get myself ready,
quiet as a sunrise.

I grab my backpack
containing
the essentials—
extra clothes,
just in case;
my drumsticks,
just because;
my camera,
just for fun;
and a box of jelly beans,
just like always.

I s l i n k
into the dark kitchen,
clutching the note
I wrote last night.

        I thought of everything.

The note goes in front
of the food-splattered
Betty Crocker Cookbook
that sits on a stand
in the middle of the counter,
like a revered queen on her throne.

The hardest part
is unlocking the door,
walking out,
and leaving it all behind me.

There's a moment
when the dead bolt clicks
and I

freeze,

waiting to hear
if footsteps
will follow.

The footsteps don't come,

so I go.

practice makes perfect, I hope

So long.
Good-bye.
See ya later.

Every day
for the past month,
when I've left the house,
I've tried to pretend
it was *the* day.

So long, Mom.
I'll think of you
when I watch movies,
see birds in the sky,
and read all your motherly notes
that I've saved over the years.

Good-bye, Kelly.
I'll think of you
when I hear a violin's song,
see a pile of library books,
and remember all the secrets we've whispered
since we were small.

And even though
he doesn't live here anymore,
I still say to him,
See ya later, Dad.
I'll think of you
when I hear about the latest techie gadget,
watch a Mariners' game,
and bravely confront the spiders
you used to battle for me.

Today I think the words.

Tomorrow they'll expect me to say them.
I hope I can say them.

good morning

The chilly air
slides its arms around
my warm, anxious body,
and as I breathe in
its faint floral scent,
I feel myself begin
to relax.

While Mom watched
the news last night,
I stayed and watched too,
instead of retreating
to my drum set.
The weatherman said
it's supposed to be nice today.
A sunny day in March,
a rare treat for Oregon.
Next week is spring break.

It'll be raining by then.

Sure as Mom will be
curled up on the sofa
with her afghan,
drinking tea by the gallon,
watching movie after movie,
and hoping,
wishing,
praying for an escape
from the heartbreak,
it will
r
a
i
n

I walk down the sidewalk
of Englewood Avenue.
Ten years of memories
line the street
and wave.

Images
of riding bikes,
jumping rope,
playing hide-and-seek
swarm my brain
like bees.

        I shake my head and walk faster.

When I turn the corner,
the limousine is waiting.

The driver says, "Good morning."
My response to him
is quick and awkward,
the way it is
when I have to say
those words to someone
I don't know.

And then I tell myself,
You better get used to it.

Three years ago

Dear Amber,

*It breaks our hearts that you don't want to meet us.
We are hurt, but we also understand that it is a big
shock. Perhaps you just need more time to get used
to the idea.*

*We think about you every day, and have so many
questions for you. What do you look like? What
activities do you enjoy? What foods are your favorite?*

*I will tell you a little bit about us, and maybe as we
move toward meeting one another, it will help you to
not be so afraid.*

*The most important thing to know about me is that I
love children. I have been a child-care provider for over
twenty years. I get notes from parents telling me those
first children I cared for years ago are now doing well
in college!*

Allen also loves children, and has spent his life working in the educational system, as a teacher, a vice principal, and now, for the past few years, a principal. He is the kindest man you'll ever meet. He has a big heart with a huge capacity to love.

We'd love to hear from you. Please write back? I've enclosed our contact information along with our picture. I thought you might be curious about us the way we are curious about you.

We really hope to hear from you.

Love,

Jeanie and Allen

only good things

I don't have to tell the driver
where we're going.
He knows.
I arranged this weeks ago.

Since there's no bus
that goes to the beach,
my choices were
a taxi or a limo.
I chose the limo
because the next
twenty-four hours
are not about
holding back,
being cheap,
thinking hard,
taking crap,
feeling bad.

They're about
being me,
loving life,
finding joy,
playing hard,
taking risks,
and who knows what else.

To plan it all
would take away from
the fun and excitement
of what's to come.

Let the day
reveal itself to me
in its own time,
in its own way.

I am yours, Today.

I am yours.

there is only one sky

As we head west,
the sun begins to rise
behind us,
turning the sky
sweet shades
of pink and orange.

The sky makes me think
of my mother.

When, as a curious five-year-old, I asked her
why she chose my name,
she explained
Amber means "sky"
in another language.

"You, sweetheart,"
she told me,
"you are my sky."

I remember her answer
because I didn't know
what it meant
to be someone's sky.

As I stare out at
the body of blueness
splashed with orange,
pink, and white streaks,
so magnificent
I want to tuck the entire
masterpiece into my bag
and keep it forever,

        I finally understand.

my mom

If I am her sky,
she is my sun.

Warm,
bright,
and
ever present.

Even in the darkness,
I am comforted knowing
she is there,
always there,
even if I can't see her
or feel her.

While I play
loud and strong
on my drums,
she walks
quiet and soft
in the woods.

She looks for birds,
marks them in her book,
and finds joy in
discovering the new.

Peace and quiet,
two things she loves.
Noise and rhythm,
two things I love.

But as the sky
and the sun coexist,
each needing the other,
it's the same with
me and my mom.

Sometimes, love is loud.
Sometimes, love is quiet.

Always, love is my mom.

not today

I wipe a tear away
and remind myself
I'm not riding
in a hearse.
This is a limo.
My limo.
And this day
is supposed to be
my day.

I grab my jelly beans,
fish one out,
and pop it in my mouth
without looking.

I play my guess-the-flavor game
whenever I think
too much,
too long,
or, like today,
at all.

Because when you
put something
on your tongue,
your mind focuses
on it almost
instantaneously.

First one.
Cotton candy.

And then another.
Very cherry.

It brings me
back to the moment,
and I want to live
the moment with everything I've got.

I grab a glass
and fill it with
sparkling water
because that's all there is,
and besides,
me and alcohol
don't mix.

One leads to two
leads to too many.
I tend to lean
toward extreme,
and I don't like
where I end up
after I start down
that road.

I raise my glass
and toast to no one
and to everyone.

       "To a good day," I say out loud.

I drink the water,
the fizzy bubbles

sk ip pi ng

across my tongue.

That's more like it.

sorry, Mom

As we drive
the tree-lined highway
toward my destination,
I wait for the inevitable.

When my phone rings,
I can see the panic in her eyes,
hear the fear in her voice,
feel the longing in her heart.
They are friends of mine—
panic, fear, longing.

I send her
to voice mail
so I can talk to my new friends
for today—
joy, happiness, and adventure.

"Hi, Mom.
I'm sorry I left so early.
I didn't want tears this morning.
There will be enough of that
tomorrow.
I hope you understand.
This is the last day
of my before.
The day before it all changes.
Forever.

This is my day.

I promise I'll call you
if anything comes up.
But I'll be okay.
Try not to miss me too much.

After all,
it's
just

one

day.

I love you.
Amber."

how it has to be

These past weeks,
Mom has hovered close,
asking me to help her
with this thing,
that thing,
and another thing.

Today, I just couldn't help her.

She's a crier.
Watching movies—
kind of our thing—
she'll cry whether
it's a happy ending
or a sad ending.

Today, I had to help myself.

If we were together,
I'm afraid it would be one
long,
painful,
miserable day
of crying.

She'll call my dad in tears.
Tell him I've left.
He'll come over.
They'll let Kelly stay home
from middle school.
They'll be a family together,
without me.

> Today, they'll have to help
> themselves.

And to their surprise,
they'll survive.

fill my soul

My iPod,
tucked away
in my backpack,
is my only true
companion today.

Of course,
she brings along
the music
I love
with my whole
heart.

When I put the
earbuds in,
I find P!nk
still singing
about wanting
an endless night.

I lean back
into the cool leather seat,
close my eyes,
and let the music fill
all the empty spaces

with glitter.

missing you, Madison

Although the ocean
never sleeps,
the town of Newport does,
and now,
in the early morning hours,
it's barely awake.

The driver drops me off
at a café.
Inside I order hot tea
and a donut, and take a seat
with a view.

Two older ladies
sit across the room,
drinking and talking,
one of them tall and skinny
with a neck like a giraffe,
the other so chubby,
she has three chins
and no neck at all.

What a pair.

It makes me think
of Madison,
and my chest responds
with a dull ache.

We're as different
as country music and hip-hop.
She's cute and sweet
with wavy blond hair.
I'm rough around the edges
with red dye bleeding
through my naturally brown hair.
She likes the rainbow colors.
I like the scary colors.
She sings in musicals,
I play in a rock band.
She has other girl friends,
I have other boy friends.

Except for Madison.

Because the things that matter to us,
that's what we have in common.
We like hanging downtown,
eating sushi, talking books,
politics, and school drama,
loving it when we see eye-to-eye
and loving it even more when we don't.

Art makes us smile,
and on summer days when
there's nothing else to do,
we are Monet and Picasso,
the street our canvas
and chalk our paintbrush
of choice.

She's a one-in-a-million friend,
and I'm lucky she's mine.

How can I live without her?

I thought about asking
her to come with me today.
I thought, maybe I
could make her promise
to keep a smile on that
adorable face of hers
no matter what.

But the more I thought about it,
the more I decided I'd be asking
the impossible.

Like asking a soldier
to not feel any fear
before heading into battle.
I've already slipped once,
and I'm the one
who has the most to gain
in keeping my own promise.

It's better this way.

A little lonelier.
But better.

morning waves

After I've emptied
my tea cup, I head
to the beach.

The white caps slide across
the sparkly blue dance floor.
They whisper to me,
Join us—dance!

I close my eyes,
take a deep breath of the sea air,
and spin around and around,
the sand cold yet soothing
underneath my bare feet.

When I stop,
the world is spinning,
and I gasp at how
familiar it is.

Everything spinning out of control.

When my balance is back,
I run, faster and faster,
jumping over seaweed
strewn out on the sand
like strands
of a mermaid's hair.

I run past an old man
on a morning walk,
waking up to the smell
of salty air instead of
fresh brewed coffee.

Into the water I walk,
my pants rolled
up to my knees.
I stand still
and let the cold waves
splash over my feet.

It feels good.

Something *finally* feels
good.

like a painful song

The waves
          come and go.

          I know that rhythm.

I know it too well.

Like the anger,
          sadness,
          denial

I've felt
these past weeks
that I've been pushing down,
telling myself to
suck it up—
it all comes back.

          Bigger.

          Stronger.

I walk out farther,
the water almost
knee-high.

My eyes close
for a moment
and my heart wishes
I could throw it all
to the tide,
like a bottle
with a scribbled note inside.

And then,
without warning,
a big wave comes
and splashes me,
as if to make a point.

The waves never stop.
No matter how much
I wish they would,
the waves
                    come and go
                            come and go
                                    come and go.

Two years, nine months ago

Dear Amber,

How are you doing, honey? We haven't heard back
from you, but that's okay. We'll keep writing. Maybe
the more you get to know about us, the more you'll see
that we are good people. Allen says you are probably
afraid. And of course, that's understandable. You have
no idea what kind of people we are. But through these
letters, I hope you'll see there's nothing to fear.

A newspaper reporter knocked on our door yesterday.
I wonder if the same was true for you? I know this will
probably be disruptive to your life. I wish it didn't have
to be that way, but we don't know what else to do.
We want to know you so badly—to have a relationship
with you.

Today was a beautiful spring day, so I went for a long
walk in our neighborhood. The tulips are starting to
bloom. I love tulips. We have lots of red and yellow ones
planted in our front yard. They're my favorite flower.

I'm wondering, what's yours?

Love,
Jeanie and Allen

treasure hunt

I sit in the cool sand,
my mind drifting
like wood on water.

A few years ago
we stayed at a beach house,
Dad, Mom, Kelly, and I.

When we were almost ready to head home,
Mom insisted the three of us get
one last fill of the ocean,
as if we were fragile sea creatures,
needing the water
to survive.

When we got down to the beach,
Dad started running and said,
"Ten minutes to find a treasure.
The winner of the best treasure
gets to pick the music for the ride home."

Kelly yelled out,
"I'm winning this one, Jelly!"

I threw my head back and laughed.

We hadn't played Treasure Hunt
since Kelly and I were little.

We used to play all the time—
at the park,
on a hike,
even in our own backyard.

I skipped across the sand, the breeze
catching my shirt,
exposing my belly, white
as a seagull's.

                    I laughed again.

Across the beach,
Dad and Kelly
scoured the wet sand,
no doubt searching for
one of Mother Nature's
lost jewels.

My eyes scanned
the dry sand
by the piles of driftwood.
I dug with my hands,
searching for
a buried treasure,
until my arms
became heavy.

I climbed the pile,
searching the other side,
and then
something glistened
in the sun:
a blue-and-silver fishing lure
complete with a hook.

An amazing treasure,
especially since I was saving someone
from being caught in the foot.

Dad waved his arms,
telling us time
was up.
Kelly showed us her find first:
a golden rock, an agate,
clear and smooth.

When I showed them mine, Dad said,
"An in-line spinner.
Very nice!"

And then, with his fists closed tight,
he turned his hands over and slowly
spread his fingers
wide   open
like a sea anemone
in a tide pool.

Kelly and I gasped
when we saw
what he held.

Two silver chains
with a tiny
silver dollar charm
on the end of each one.

After Kelly—always the affectionate child—
gave him a hug,
she said, "But you don't win, right?
You didn't find it.
The rules are you have to find it."

Affectionate *and* competitive.

"Kel, I think we both win.
Thanks, Dad.
I love it."

"Me, too,"
Kelly echoed.
"But who picks the—"

I tapped her on the shoulder
and yelled, "You're it!"
intentionally ending one game
and beginning another.
Of course she chased me,
because that's what little sisters do.
And of course I let her choose
the music on the car ride home,
because that's what big sisters do.

They let their
little sisters
win.

mixed feelings

I like

the memories
because they remind me
I haven't always been
this girl,
constantly
mad or scared
or confused.

I don't like

the memories
because the tears
come easily,
and once again I break
my promise
to myself for this day.

It's a constant battle.

A war between
remembering   and forgetting.

my heroes

I catch a cab at ten
and make my way
to the aquarium.

I want to look at sharks,
quiet and
fierce.

Study them.
Learn from them.

They own the water.

                They are not afraid.

beautiful boy

He stares
at the tank
of jellyfish.

I stand on the other side
and watch
the pale pink parachutes
        glide
through the water.

They are

hypnotic.

He moves
slowly,
circling the
round tank.

Moving closer
to me.

I realize
I'm not watching
the jellyfish anymore.

        I'm watching him watching them.

He stares
with such intensity,
I can't help but wonder,
What is he thinking?
Feeling?
Wishing?

While he's under their spell,
I take him in.
He's wearing a black knit beanie
with bits of black hair
sticking out,
a gray hoody,
and skinny jeans.

Only skinny people
can get away
with wearing
skinny jeans,
which is why
I don't own a pair.
Short-and-stocky jeans
are more my style.

So, he's skinny.
But not gross skinny.
Good skinny.
Cute skinny.

His warm voice
tiptoes into the
quiet room.

"Did you see that movie?" he asks.

I did.
Without asking,
I know he's talking
about *Seven Pounds*.

My mom is crazy
for Will Smith.
She dragged me along
like a box of Junior Mints
as soon as it hit
the theaters.

I was haunted
for days.

"Yes," I tell him.
"A crazy way to die."

He's standing right next to me.

We both watch
the glowing jellies,
perhaps imagining
reaching in and touching them,
threads of fire
burning our skin.

"I don't know," he says.
"They look so delicate. Pretty.
Prettier than a gun.
Or a rope."

I look at him.
"Didn't anyone tell you
looks aren't everything?"

like

"Cade," he says, sticking out his hand.

"Amber," I say, accepting his offer.
The warmth is a shock.
A tremor scurries
down my spine.

"You from around here?" he asks.

"Salem."

He nods.

"You?" I ask.

"Portland."

He smiles.
"So. You like jellyfish?"

I bite my lip
to keep from laughing.
Is he going to order me one
like a cheeseburger?

"I love them."

"Me too."

What is he,
a great white
circling his prey?

I don't think I care.

something special

Cade motions
with a nod
to follow him.

He's holding the pole,
and I'm the
fish on the line.

Just how far
will he pull me
in?

Around the corner
only a few kids
are at the
tidal pool touch tank.

My heart's racing,
but not from what's
in the tank.

With names like
pencil sea urchin,
scarlet hermit crab,
and chocolate chip sea star,
the creatures
all sound friendly.

I reach into the cold water.

The back of a starfish
feels like wet sandpaper
against my fingertips.

Cade pets it too, his
fingers almost
touching
mine.

"When I was little," he says,
"I wanted to take them home.
Turn my bathtub into a touch pool."

It makes me smile because
I was the same way.

Sea stars
are

m*a*g*i*c*a*l.

We wish on stars,
millions of miles away, and
yet here we can *touch* them.

I've never wished
on a sea star before,
but I want to try it.

I hold my breath and make a wish.

As he gives the
starfish a final pet,
his fingers graze mine.
Just barely.
But they do.

And the way I feel
when it happens,
I know I made
the right wish.

Please don't let me go quite yet.

ah, to be a snail

Next to me,
a girl tugs on my jacket.

Her eyes round as sand dollars,
she asks me, "Why is that shell moving?"
She points to the water where
a shell appears to slide across the tank
by an invisible force.

"That's a hermit crab.
There's a crab underneath the shell.
He carries it with him wherever he goes."

She smiles with relief.
"A shell for a home? Lucky!"

I think about that.

A shell,
all his own,
no one arguing,
you belong here
or there, with us
or with them.

Yeah.
I'd have to agree.
Pretty damn lucky.

secrets

"No school today?" the volunteer asks
from the other side of the display.

I jump.

I want to tell her
school is the least
of my worries.

But I don't respond.
And neither does Cade.
Sometimes you just don't want
to explain yourself.

She's curious
the way a nosy neighbor
is curious,
bringing cookies over,
asking questions,
trying to get the dirt.

Well, I'm not sharing.

And apparently
Cade isn't either.

He turns
and walks
away.

I follow,
my resolve
to spend the day alone
softer than I originally
thought.

a keen observation

Outside
we watch
as sea otters
swim and play
in their small
aquarium world.

One otter
paddles around
on his back,
spinning a blue ball
on his tummy.

I could watch them
for hours.

                Because they get it.

They get that
life is short and
you should just
forget the crap
and have fun.

Another otter
comes to play
and the ball
is batted away.

Around and around
they twirl through
the water together,
like little boys wrestling.

"That's the way to live, huh?" Cade says.

I guess he gets it too.

Two years, six months ago

Dear Amber,

What a week it's been. I took two new babies into my day care this week—twins! Their names are Benjamin and Bryce. I've never cared for twins before. It's a bit of a challenge. But they are beautiful, and they smile often. If you've ever held a smiling baby, you know there's nothing quite like it. You are still the most important part of their world. Once they start rolling over, crawling, walking, their world expands, and suddenly, you just aren't as important. It's how it should be, of course. But it always makes me a little sad.

Over the past few months, most of my families have left me. I was sad to see the children I care for so much leave. But I'm trying to be understanding and supportive—they have to do what's best for them and their families. I'm thankful to have the twins here now. And Sierra, a two-year-old. She's my sunshine.

I know not everyone will agree with what we are doing. I also understand that people don't want to get caught up in the drama. I've asked the media to respect our privacy, but they obviously don't care.

I suppose the one good thing was that we were finally able to see a picture of you on the news. Did you notice how much you look like Allen?

You are beautiful.

Love,

Jeanie and Allen

shocking

Next we head to the exhibit
I most want to see.

Passages of the Deep.

Sharks and stingrays swim
above us,
below us,
all around us.

We walk through
the tunnel of glass
slowly,
as if we're afraid
of falling in.

"Can you feel it?" Cade asks me.

"Feel what?"

"The power.
The confidence.
They're so damn confident."

I nod.
I do feel it.
But I want to tell him,
I feel something else too.

Electricity.

And it's not from
the eels.

never before

Guys always look at me
and see the cool girl
who plays drums,
and they think,
friend.

Right now,
I want to know
what this guy thinks.
I want to know
what this guy feels.

I want to know

        this guy.

trapped

He stops.
Touches the glass.
Looks up
at a leopard shark
swimming
over and back,
over and back,
over and back.

"Look at him," he says.
"He owns that water.
Nothing bothers him.
Nothing.
He's free to swim and do
whatever the hell he wants.
Man. I want to be like that."

"Cade?"

"Yeah?"

                    "He's trapped in a tank."

The shark swims
right past us.
If it weren't
for the glass, we'd be
fingers to fins.

"Oh, God," he whispers.
"Let him go."

radio for help

Why do I get the feeling
this boy is
lost at sea?

Just like me?

what a feeling

We stay with the sharks
for a long time,
maybe hoping
they will fill us up
with all the power
and confidence they possess.

Or maybe it's more than that.

People pass through,
lavishing the creatures
with praise and admiration.

And yet,
as much as visitors
appreciate them,
maybe even love them,
there are boundaries
and they're respected—
no questions asked.

So here,
in the passages of the deep,
among the deadliest creatures,
for just a moment, one
incredible,
miraculous
moment,
I feel

safe.

hold on

When we're
alone for a few minutes,
we stand side by side,
watching a bat ray skim
against the glass like a flying carpet.

It fascinates me.
Then something
even more fascinating.

"I'm hungry," Cade says.
"Wanna grab some lunch?"

I look at him.
Really look,
as his eyes stay fixed
on mine.

His eyes are deep brown.

Deep like a good conversation.
Deep like a hole.
Deep, of course, like
the ocean.

I fall in.
I say yes.

ninety-nine degrees

I count
in my mind
the number of words
I've said
to this guy.

Twenty?
Twenty-five?

            Either way, not many.

And even now
as we walk, the only sound
either of us makes
is the sound of our shoes
hitting asphalt.

We step
in rhythm,
and in my mind
I come in with
a drum fill that makes
the crowd go wild.

He looks at me.
Smiles.
I smile back.
And still, no words.

One time Mom told me the people
you can be quiet with
are the ones
you are the most
comfortable with.

Then why am I sweating
like a lobster headed for
a boiling pot?

spread the luck

Cade reaches to the ground,
picks up a penny,
puts it in his pocket.

"Short on cash?" I tease.

"Short on luck," he quips back.

                    Maybe he'll share with me.

well . . . we both watch movies

He drives
a classic, pale yellow
VW Beetle.

It's as cool as he is.

Now it's my turn.

"Did you see that movie?"

He looks at me
over the top of the car.
I hold my eyes steady,
not wanting to give it away.

It's old.
One of Mom's favorites.
I didn't really get the appeal.
But I liked the guy's car.
A car just like this car.

"Yeah," he says.
"What a crazy town.
I mean, seriously?
No music?"

Oh my God.
He knew.
Footloose.
He knew the one.

I'm impressed.
And I'm not impressed easily.
Sometimes, not at all.

But today?
Definitely impressed.

off-limits

Sitting in his car,
I wonder if he
can hear my heart
beating loud and hard,
the way I like
my music.

When he turns the key,
Fall Out Boy plays
loud and hard,
the way Cade likes
his music.

He reaches for the volume.
His hand is shaking.
Just a little bit.
But I see it.
And I know
I'm not the only one
feeling like we're on the edge
of a cliff,

                about to jump.

His brown eyes stare into mine.
"One condition," he says.
"For today."

"Okay."

"We don't ask each other
what we're both doing here.
At the beach, by ourselves.
I won't ask you.
You don't ask me."

I nod. "Great."

"Great," he says as he puts the car
in reverse.

Even though I'm dying to know.

observant

"What do you like?" he asks.
"I mean, in music."

"Anything and everything.
Almost, anyway.
The White Stripes are my favorite.
Meg White is pretty much my hero.
But I also love P!nk.
I mean, music that touches my soul?
P!nk all the way.
And, she's so damn cool."

"You and her,
you have something in common."

"Tough on the outside,
tender on the inside?"

"Well, maybe," he says,
"but I wouldn't really know."

I feel my cheeks get warm,
like when I'm playing with
the band and I miss a beat.

"You both have a color for a name."

Right.
That.

special

On the Oregon coast,
Mo's is the place
for bowls of clam chowder
with paprika sprinkled on top,
and warm bread
with a flaky, golden crust.

Picnic benches line
the wall of windows
overlooking the bay.

We're seated in the corner.

He takes his hat off and
scratches his head.

Even with his hair
sticking out every which way,
he's cute.

He tries to pat it down,
grinning sheepishly at me.

"It's fine," I say.

"Yeah?"

"Yeah."

"I like the red," he says.
"In yours."

"Thanks. My mom isn't a fan."

He reaches for his glass of water.
"Mothers can be a pain in the ass."

I shrug.
"Mine's all right.
Most of the time."

"Does she know you're here?" he asks.

"Sort of. You?"

"No one knows where I am right now."
He leans in just a little.

His smile lights me up.

"Except you."

my turn

"Let's play four truths and a lie," I say
after we give the waitress our order.

"Okay.
You go first."

I take a deep breath.
For some unknown reason,
I want him to know.

I want it out there
so I don't have to work
at hiding it from him
all day long.

I imagine those sharks.
Strong.
Confident.
Not afraid.

"I'm scared to drive.
I was switched at birth.
I collect albums and own an old turntable.
Someday I'll be a nuclear physicist.
Jelly beans are my favorite candy."

He doesn't even
flinch.

"You don't seem like the
nuclear physicist type."

My face must be
the portrait
of surprise.

He smiles.
Tilts his head.
"I got it right?"

"Yeah."

"Cool.
Okay," he says.
"Let me think on mine for a second."

And that's it.
No interrogation.
No sympathy.
Not even an uncomfortable moment.

Seriously?

Two years, three months ago

Dear Amber,

*Did you have a happy birthday? We hope you
enjoyed the flowers we sent you for your special day.*

*We visited the cemetery, and put roses on Charlotte's
grave. Purple ones. Oh, how she loved the color purple.*

*I remember we bought her a doll for her fourth birthday.
She opened it up and started to cry. "What's wrong?" we
asked her. "Her dress is red," she told us. "I hate red! Her
dress should be purple!" After that, I learned how to make
doll clothes.*

*Charlotte was quite opinionated—a strong-willed
child. I suppose some might call it stubborn. Although
she challenged our parenting skills at times, it was so
much fun watching her grow up. She was never afraid
to try the unknown or conquer the unfamiliar. When she
got sick, she fought it with everything she had. She fought
so hard, we thought for sure she'd win, just like she did
with the purple dress.*

Over the years, she grew to have quite the doll collection. I still have them. The other day, I brought some of them out and let Sierra play with them. She was in heaven.

What about you? Did you play with dolls when you were young? What's your favorite color? Do you enjoying trying new things?

Won't you please write back and tell us?

Love,
Jeanie and Allen

his turn

"I write songs everywhere I go.
I love macaroni and cheese.
My dog's name is Boo.
I'm scared of hospitals.
I love the ocean so much, I would live and die at sea if I
could."

I study him as he
says each one.
But I can't read him,
and besides,
I'm only thinking
one thing—
Please be a songwriter,
please be a songwriter,
please be a songwriter.

"Your dog's name isn't Boo."

"It is."

"Shit.
Uh, you don't love the ocean *that* much."

"Yeah. I do."

If he's not a songwriter, I'll cry!

"Do you hate macaroni and cheese?" I whisper.

"Unlike the majority of America, yes."

What a relief.
Then I have to know.

"Are you writing a song today?
I mean, do you have words?
Or an idea?"

He nods.
"Like I said, everywhere I go."

Underneath the table,
I pinch my leg,
to be sure
I'm not dreaming.

And what do you know, I'm not.

As the waitress sets
our food in front of us,
I try to figure out
what the other truths mean.

I want to ask.
But I follow his lead,
letting the questions
float up and away
toward the rafters,
like the steam
from our bowls of soup.

no place better

We eat our lunch
and talk about school
and what we're missing.

At first
it's serious stuff.

me: A test in Chemistry.
A self-portrait in Art.

him: A speech in Language Arts.
A meeting with his guidance counselor.

me: Looks of pity in the hallway.

him: Lack of understanding.

When he pushes his bowl
away, I know it's time
to push away
the serious stuff too.

me: Rubber chicken nuggets.

him: Pizza drowning in grease.

me: Stressed-out teachers.

him: Teachers who don't give a damn.

I look out the window and
imagine the warm sun on my face,
the sound of the surf in my ears.

                    "I'm glad I'm not there."

I feel his eyes on me.
"I'm glad I'm here," he says.

I'm no longer
just thinking warm thoughts.
I'm feeling them.

gonna build us some fun

After lunch
we stroll through
a souvenir shop.

Shells in all
shapes and sizes.
Sand dollars,
whole and perfect,
not broken,
how I always find them.
Taffy in a
kaleidoscope
of colors.

Cade grabs a couple
of plastic shovels and buckets.
I go for a bag of
assorted saltwater taffy.

A wave of giddiness
washes over me
because we'll
play on the beach
with no other thoughts than
                have fun,
                        have fun,
                                have fun.

I start to give him money,
but he takes the taffy
and pushes away the bills.
"I've got it."

"But—"

"No. Please."
He smiles.
"Let me do this, okay?
It's good for my ego."

Before I can argue,
my phone rings.

It's Madison.
I've ignored
all of her texts.

She's probably worried,
so I step away.

"Hey."

"Amber, why aren't you at school?
Where are you?"

"Newport."

"What? Why?
Will you be back soon?"

"No. Not until tomorrow."

"Tomorrow?
But Amber, you—"

"Look, I can't do this now, okay?
I gotta go. I'm fine. Better than fine.
I'll see you tomorrow."

"Everything all right?" Cade asks.

I take a shovel from his hands.

"Nothing a sand castle won't cure."

from nothing comes greatness

Bucket
after bucket
after bucket
filled with
cool,
damp
sand.

Walls
and towers.

More walls.
Some turrets.
A staircase.

He builds
a staircase
for the castle!

Windows
and doors.

A castle
truly built
for a king.

I may not know
a lot about this guy,
but one thing
I do know?

He knows his way
around a sand castle.

waiting to be rescued

When Kelly and I
built a sand castle together,
we'd dig a moat around it.

Then we'd sit back,
waiting for the tide
to come in.

Once, we imagined
we were princesses,
stuck in the towers,
waiting for princes
to rescue us.

But moats filled with
crocodiles
make rescues
difficult.

"My prince has a flying horse," Kelly'd announced.

And just like that, she'd won. She was free.

I couldn't think of a way to be rescued.
Not one.

So I, the pissed-off princess,
kicked the castle walls,
causing them to come
crashing down.

Even then
I hated impossible
situations.

surprise

Sisterly memories
cause bittersweet emotions
to surface.

Kelly looks nothing like me,
acts nothing like me,
is really *nothing* like me.

But she's my sister.
And that means
everything.

I retreat with my bag
to a large piece of driftwood
and take a seat.

I close my eyes
and breathe in the soothing
smell of salty ocean air.

Seagulls cry
in the distance,
as if they are lonely
despite the company
of a beach full of people.

I know that cry.

"Keep your eyes closed," Cade whispers.
"And open your mouth."

Of course
I immediately
open my eyes.

He sits next to me.
"Come on."
He smiles.
"Don't you trust me?"

I want to trust him.
I close my eyes.
And I slowly
open

my mouth.

There is sweetness
with a hint of salt,
and the distinctive texture
of taffy.

"Guess what flavor," he asks.

I smile.
He's playing my game.

           How did he know my game?

"Lemon."

I open my eyes.

He's chewing too.

"Mine's lime."

Two of my favorites.

secret revealed

"Where'd you learn how to do that?" I ask.

"Guess taffy flavors?" he teases.

I nudge him with my elbow.

"No.
Build a sand castle."

"My dad.
We spend a lot of time at the beach.
He lives here in Newport."

"You live with your mom?"

He starts digging in the sand,
and I wonder
if the questions
are getting too personal.

He nods. "My parents are divorced."

"Mine too," I say.

He pauses.
Stops digging,
and our eyes meet.

"Yeah. I know."

"What? How?"

Wait.
Of course.
The news.
It's been national for a while.

He goes back to making
his hole in the sand.

"Did you know it was me?" I ask.
"When you first saw me, did you know?"

He shakes his head.
"You looked familiar.
But I couldn't place you.
Until lunch."

Two little kids
with their mom
stop to admire
our sand castle.
I'm thankful
for the momentary
distraction.

The kids look
as if they wish
they could shrink
to the size of tiny crabs
and climb inside.

I wish I could climb inside.

Me, the princess,
and Cade, the prince,
saving me from Jeanie and Allen,
the big,
bad
dragons.

"When do you leave?" he asks.

I barely get the word out.
"Tomorrow."

And then I reach
for another piece
of taffy.

the story

Four
unsuspecting parents.
Two
newborn baby girls.
One
incredibly busy night
in a small hospital.

Accidents happen.

For ten years
no one is the wiser.

Until one day
the unthinkable happens.
One of the girls, Charlotte,
comes down with
leukemia.

When her parents
are tested for a
possible blood transfusion,
the results are shocking.

Their blood types don't match.

They don't tell Charlotte.
The stress would be too much.
They simply love her
and make her comfortable
until the very end,
which comes faster
than anyone had predicted.

Most stories would end there.
Okay, maybe after the
sorry-ass hospital is sued
for millions of dollars.
But not this story.
Hell, no.

Charlotte's parents,
Allen and Jeanie, try
to pull themselves
out of the nightmare
they've been living
by searching for
their biological child.

They want to find her.
They want to meet her.
They want to *know* her.

In a surprise decision
the judge is sympathetic
to the bereaved couple,
and she awards
shared custody.

Six months with one family.
Six months with the other.

                    I close my eyes and breathe.

The taffy rolls around on my tongue.
Strawberry.
My mom's favorite.

My only mom's favorite.

One year, six months ago

Dear Amber,

I want to share something a reporter asked me recently, and my answer, because it occurred to me that you may be wondering the same thing.

He asked, "Are you trying to replace one daughter with another?"

I told the reporter, absolutely not. No one can take Charlotte's place. She was our daughter, the girl we loved and raised. The girl with the beautiful smile and the sparkly aqua eyes. The girl who loved the stage and dreamed of being an actress. The girl who loved animals and decided to become a vegetarian when she was eight. She was the light of our life. When we learned we weren't her biological parents, it didn't change how much we loved her.

But ever since we discovered you're out there, we've felt like something is missing. Like a piece of ourselves is missing. I'm sure your parents feel the same way, but unfortunately, they don't have the chance to get to know their other daughter like we do.

We weren't able to have any more children after Charlotte was born, although we wanted to. But now, we have the opportunity to get to know you. The opportunity to love you!

We know you can't take Charlotte's place. No one can. Still, Amber, we are family. For better, for worse, you are connected to us.

We want you in our life, because family is everything.

Love,
Jeanie and Allen

no choice

My parents
didn't fight it.

The financial
and emotional
stress
that an appeal
would bring—
they couldn't
fight it.

"It's not that long
until you're eighteen,"
Dad told me.
"Hang in there
until then.

            You can choose then."

Not now.
Then.

My friends
always want to know
what I think about it.

Reporters have asked me
how I feel about it.

Like it matters.

It doesn't matter.

The decision's been made.
I'm going.
End of case.
End of story.

Except it's not.
Not for me anyway.
For me, it's just the beginning.

where'd that come from?

Cade doesn't say any more.
He doesn't ask any more.
We made a deal, after all.

It's a funny thing, though.

Part of me wishes he would.

lucky me

My bag
is still open.

I reach for my camera.

"Can I take your picture?" I ask him.
"Next to the castle?"

He gets up,
offers me his hand,
and I take it.
I stand.

I start to pull my hand away,
but he
doesn't
let
go.

Oh my God,
is this really happening?
It feels like a stingray
is swimming around
in my stomach.

With his other hand
he reaches into his pocket
and takes out the
lucky penny.

"Heads, you can take it.
Tails, you can't."

He flips it
high in the air
and lets it land
on the sand.

We bend down
to see what Chance
has to say.

Heads.
Hallelujah, it's heads.

Except,
he has to let go
of my hand
so I can take the picture.

                Still, I want it.

I want to remember
the amazing castle
I made with the boy
who seems to get
more amazing
by the minute.

more than just pictures

Mom gave me
a camera
for my birthday.

I take pictures,
print them,
and put them in scrapbooks,
where I write notes
and draw art
on the pages.

For each page,
I cut and paste
pieces of my heart.

In the coming months,
I will hold on to
those pieces,
even when it feels like
there's no part
of my heart

left.

spooked

After I take Cade's picture,
he stares at our beautiful
sand creation
for the longest time.
Like he sees ghosts
hiding there.

I leave him alone
and go to work
covering my feet
and legs with sand.

Soon he   marches   across   the   castle.

No more towers.
No more walls.
No more staircase.

I get it.

Sometimes
you want to remember.

And sometimes
you need to forget.

tell me your story

Many times
when I read a book,
I want to savor
each word,
each phrase,
each page,
loving the prose
so much,
I don't want it
to end.

Other times
the story pulls me in,
and I can hardly
read fast enough,
the details flying by,
some of them lost
because all that matters
is making sure
the character
is all right
when it's over.

This day
is like the best
of both kinds
of books.

I want to cherish
each moment and yet,
I've got to know
that this character
named Cade
will be okay
when this story
ends.

sinking

"Cade?"

He glances my way,
then walks toward
the ocean.

Did I see the start of tears?

I run after him.
"Hey." I grab his arm.
"Are you okay?"

I pull on him
so he'll stop.

"You can talk to me," I tell him.
"Please?"

He's quiet for a minute.
His eyes are on the water
before they turn toward me.

"You should go," he says.
"Go and have your fun day.
I'll just ruin it."

It's like he's tied an anchor
to my heart and I can feel it
dropping
down,
down,
down
to the bottom of my stomach.

"No. Hey, come on.
You aren't ruining anything.
I'm sorry.
You don't have to tell me anything.
Come on. Let's go make more fun."

Cade's eyes seek out the ocean again,
like he'll find the answer there.

So I stand there and wait,
hoping the crashing waves
and the crying gulls
will drown out the voices
in his head.

Except for mine, of course.

whatever it takes

Finally
I get my answer.

He takes my hand,
and we head back
toward our piece
of driftwood.

We go slowly,
and I wait—
for whatever
he might want to tell me.

"No more pictures, okay?"

His voice is soft.
Sad.
I want to wrap my arms
around him and tell him
everything will be all right,
even though I don't
know
anything.

I simply nod.

At least I have one.

          One picture will have to be enough.

Just like
one day
will have to be
enough.

yes, it's really me

When I put my camera away,
he sees my drumsticks.

He takes them out.
Looks them over.
Looks me over.

"You?" he asks.
"Really?"

I shrug.

He gives me
the biggest smile yet.
"Man, tonight, we have to—"

He stops.
"Never mind.
I don't want to tell you.
I'll show you.
Later."

And when he says, "Later"
I want to do cartwheels
across the beach
because that means
he's not getting rid of me
anytime soon.

our next destination

I ask
for the penny.

"Heads, Otter Crest.
Tails, Yaquina Bay Lighthouse."

Chance tells us
we'll be going
to see the lighthouse.

I'm not sure
if the actual lighthouse
is open to the public.

But we can look at it.
Admire its beauty.
Appreciate its grandness.

There is something
comforting
about a lighthouse.

In the dark of the night,
hold on to the light,
and you'll get
back home safely.

I need a personal lighthouse.

One year ago

Dear Amber,

I keep wishing you'd write to us. I would love to hear from you—to know what you're thinking. I hope you're not too upset with us for continuing to pursue a relationship with you.

I know it may seem odd that I keep writing to you when I haven't heard anything back. What can I say other than I'm not ready to give up quite yet. We have a lot of love in our hearts and want to be able to share it with you.

I thought in this letter, I might tell you a little about Texas. You won't find a nicer bunch of people than those in our town of Sweetwater, that's for sure. The weather's warm in the summer, warmer than Oregon. For fun, Allen enjoys golfing as there are some beautiful golf courses here, and I'm involved in a couple of clubs—a book club and a bridge club.

Sweetwater's our home, and we look forward to sharing it with you, and making it your home, too. You may be wondering how we ended up here after living in Oregon, so I'll tell you the story.

*Allen and I met at Western Oregon State College, where
we were both pursuing degrees in education. We stayed
in Oregon after we got married, because we both found
work easily, and we liked the climate. However, after
Charlotte was born, I felt a strong desire to move back
to Texas, where I'm originally from. I wanted to be
closer to my family and for Charlotte to know her
grandparents, her aunts and uncles, and her cousins.
Mostly, I wanted her to grow up knowing she was
surrounded by people who love her. So after Charlotte
turned two years old, we moved to Texas. And we've
been here ever since. What a blessing it was to be here,
with loved ones close by, when she became ill.*

*If we're granted shared custody, you'll get to see for
yourself what a wonderful place Sweetwater is.
I pray for that every day.*

*Love,
Jeanie and Allen*

not all that sweet

Sweetwater, Texas?

Where football is king
and country music is queen?

They might as well
be sending me to Mars.

through death you appreciate life

In Cade's car
I flip through
his CD case
filled with
life and love
and everything in between,
looking for something
to listen to on the ride
to the lighthouse.

Plans, by Death Cab for Cutie,
catches my eye, since it's sticking out
a little farther than the others.

Cade glances at the CD.
"Oh, no," he says.
"Not that one.
Not right now."

"Oh, yes.
Yes, yes, yes!
I Will Follow You into the Dark
is amazing. Brilliant.
I want to hear it."

When he stops
at a red light,
he turns and looks at me.

"Do you know what it's about?
The CD? Do you know what every
single song on there is about?"

I admit, I don't.
I've never listened
to the whole thing,
just the few tracks
I've downloaded.

"It's about death.
Death and dying.
Mortality and how to cope with loss."

"Really?" I ask.
"All of it?"

"All of it."

                    I put it in.

Because now
I'm curious.

don't think the worst

I ask if Cade's
ever written a song
about death.

"A few," he replies.
"Okay, more than a few."

"So you get it," I say.
"It's mysterious.
We have lots of questions, and we
want to understand.
Music helps with that."

"Music helps with everything," he says.

"True."

And as Ben Gibbard's
vocals reach
into our souls,
grabbing and
shaking the
shit out of them,
Cade says,
"It's sad.
And for one day,
one damn day,
I don't want to feel that."

His jaw is tight.
He grips the steering wheel
as he stares at the road ahead.
I study him.
Something about what
I see in his eyes,
his face,
his body language,
scares me.

It makes me wonder
if death or the thought of death
or even the wish of death
has been chasing him.

Is he running
from something?
I remember what he said.

I love the ocean so much,
I would live and die at sea if I could.

Or
running to
something?

No.
I have to believe
this day is about living,
not dying.
For both of us.

I tuck the scary
thoughts away,
just like the CD—
back where they belong.

relax

I peel
his tense fingers
on his right hand
away from
the steering wheel,
one

two

three

four

five.

With each finger,
the scowl
disappears
a little more.

When I place
his hand on
my leg
and gently
caress it,
he smiles.

That's better.

I heart ghosts

A hundred years ago
a teenager named Muriel explored
the abandoned lighthouse
with her friends.

As they were leaving,
she ran back inside
to retrieve her scarf.

                    And never came out.

When her friends searched
the lighthouse,
all they found was
a pool of blood
at the bottom of the stairs
leading up to the tower.

Some say
they've seen
and heard
strange things inside
the Yaquina Bay Lighthouse.
They think it's haunted.

I hope we see Muriel.
Or hear her.
There's nothing like a ghost
to help you forget
your own problems
for a while.

haunted indeed

It's like a postcard.

I take picture
after picture
of the white lighthouse,
almost glowing against
the baby blue backdrop
of the sky.

I don't ask Cade
to get in any of them.

But in my mind,
he's there,
in every one,
like a ghost
haunting the place.

Haunting my heart is more like it.

hold on

The lighthouse is open
for us to explore,
so we go inside.

Up the narrow
spiral stairs
we climb,
higher and higher.

We are alone,
and I think of Muriel.
Is she hiding?
Watching us?

I stop occasionally
to look down.
I take a picture,
trying to capture
the way the stairs
appear to move
in a circular manner
through the air.

Above us,
at the very top,
is the dome of glass
and the light
that shines
out to the sea.

"Dang," I say.
"No ghost."

I turn to take another picture,
and when I'm least expecting it,
Cade grabs me and says,
"Boo!"

It knocks me off balance
and I have to grab him
so I don't fall.

"I've got you," he says.

My whole body tingles.

And in that moment,
even if we're both
lost at sea,
it feels like maybe,
just maybe,
if we keep hanging on,
we'll be able
to find our way.

sorrow in the air

Back outside,
we stand
at the edge
of a cliff
and look out
at the endless supply
of blue.

It takes my breath away.

Him
and me
and the sky
and the sea.

It's like a dream.
The kind of dream
you wish for again and again,
night after night,
because it was so good
the first time.

But while my world
is momentarily
happy and dreamlike,
Cade's seems to be
gray and gloomy.

Why is it
that every time
I feel like
we're getting closer,
something causes him
to slip away?

I promised him fun,
damn it.

"Heads, glitter.
Tails, kite."

"Glitter?" he asks.

"Have you ever thrown glitter in the air?"

"No."

"Me neither.
And I want to.
P!nk says we should."

But when he flips,
it's tails.

So we'll buy a kite
and hope the mood
takes off
along with it.

Nine months ago

Dear Amber,

*We are grateful to you and your parents for the chance
to meet you. I know it wasn't easy for you.*

*When we first saw you walk into the attorney's office, we
were so happy to see you! Oh, how I wanted to give you
a hug. But I could tell you weren't ready for that. I hope
the thirty-minute meeting showed you our hearts are in
the right place.*

*Our attorney thinks we have a good chance at getting
the ruling we desire. We felt it was important for you
to hear from us personally, before the judge decides,
why we're doing this. Thank you, Amber. Thank you
for that opportunity.*

*We find it fascinating that you play the drums! If that's
your passion, we'll make sure you have what you need
here, if you come stay with us.*

We really can't wait to get to know more about you.

Take care, honey.

*Love,
Jeanie and Allen*

in the moment

Music
can change the
mood in a
drumbeat.

So I search
Cade's CDs again
for something good.

Finally I turn to
Matt Nathanson
who sings about
happy times
of love and lust.

I roll down my window.
Take a whiff of the salty air.
And hold myself back
from asking questions
that will drop us down
into a deep conversation.

As Cade drives
along the scenic highway,
we let the ocean
do the talking.
We let Matt
do the singing.
And we let ourselves
sit back and simply

listen.

that's better

At the Kite Company,
Cade says,
"You know what?
This has been a good day."

"Is it over?" I ask.

He shakes his head.
Puts his arm around me.
Smiles.
Or tries to.

"No. Thank God, no."

eight arms and
a hundred questions

Inside the shop
we see kites
in every shape and color.

"Did you see that movie?"
Cade asks.

This one is easy.
"*The Kite Runner*?
Yeah. Depressing."

An orange octopus
swims across
the ceiling.

I imagine the orange
against the sky,
bright and beautiful,
its fabricated tentacles
touching the tips
of the clouds.

I point and tell Cade,
"I want that one."

"Perfect."
As I head to the register,
a guy and a girl
come in.

Cade sees them
and tries to hide
among the dragons,
diamonds, and deltas
hanging from racks.

But it's a small store,
and difficult not to be noticed.
Cade chats with them while I pay.

When I'm done,
Cade introduces me.

"Amber, this is Parker and Emily.
My dad and Parker's dad are friends."

I smile.
"Hi. Nice to meet you."

"You, too," Parker says.

And just as I'm about
to make a lame comment
about the weather
to keep the conversation going,
Cade says, "Sorry, we gotta run.
Great to see you guys."

                    He doesn't wait for a response.

He's walking so fast,
he's practically out
the door by the time
my legs even
start moving.

"Call me!" Parker yells out.
"I'm here for you, man."

Cade waves and then
we're back in his car
with an orange octopus
that's as bright
as my ever-growing
curiosity.

20/20

Hidden, there,
behind the face
of a beautiful boy,
I see you.

The real you.

The you who flips a coin,
hoping to understand
how fate works:
this choice or that choice,
ultimately leaving you
no choice at all.

The you who smiles
and tries to be happy
because that's what
people want
you to be.

The you who plays
"it will be okay"
on repeat
all day, every day,
to try and convince
yourself
that it will be.

I see you.

Because in you,
I see me.

RSVP

"Are you going back?" he asks me.

For a second, I'm not sure what he means.
"Back where? Home?"

"Yeah. I mean, did you come here
thinking maybe you just wouldn't go back?"

I told the limo driver
to pick me up
tomorrow at eight a.m.

                    "I'm going back. I have to."

"I bet others would say *screw it,*
and just not go back."

I shrug. "Yeah. Maybe."

And that's all he says.

Wait.
Was that an invitation?

look around

This time,
Agate Beach
is our destination.

"Come on," I say,
running down the path
toward the sand,
wanting him
to run after me.

And in that moment
I close my eyes

                and I wish.

I wish
for the breeze to
blow away
our troubles.

I wish
for the sun to
dry out
our sorrow.

I wish
for the friendship
to fill up
our hearts.

I open my eyes.
Right now I see only good.

                    I want him to see it too.

release me

The kite flutters
in the wind,
and as Cade
lets the string out,
it soars
higher
and higher.

It's so calming,
watching the kite
fly in the sky.

And in this calmness
he opens up a little.

He's a senior
at Wilson High School
in Portland.
Wanted to live here with his dad,
but his mom wouldn't let him.

"It's crazy, isn't it?" I say.
"That we don't get a say.
That it doesn't matter what *we* want."

The kite dips,
and as it does,
Cade releases some string,
does a few quick maneuvers
to save it from crashing
to the ground.

It flutters again,
and soon the kite
is dancing with the sun,
back where it belongs.

"Yeah," he says. "It should matter."

holding the line

"Are you going back?" I ask him.

Because he asked me.
And maybe
that's what's on his mind.

Maybe he's here,
and he doesn't want
to go back there.

The kite dips again.

"I don't know."

This time he doesn't save it.
He lets the kite fall.

please try

After an hour
the wind dies down,
so the kite-flying
part of our day is over.

I pull out my phone
and check the clock.
My stomach's telling me
it's time to eat something.

I quickly reply to a text
from Madison,
then I'm back
to wondering
what comes next
with Cade.

"Heads, sushi," I say.
"Tails, Chinese."

"Well, it better be tails
because I don't do sushi."

"You don't do sushi?
Christ, kill me now!"

I pick up a small stick,
pretend to stab it
into my chest
and drop to the sand
on my back.

                    I lie there with my eyes closed.

Warm breath on my neck.
Soft shiver down my spine.
Sweet words whispered in my ear.

"But with you, I might try anything."

worth a shot

I turn,
his face right there.

Warm, brown eyes.
Dimple in his cheek.
Red lips, chapped from the wind.

God, he is adorable.

I want to kiss him.
But I don't.

Because more than that,
I want to know.
No, I need to know.
Is he okay?

I whisper back,
"Then please tell me what's going on with you."

soaking wet

He's up and
out of there so fast,
you'd think my words
were a cold, wet

ocean

wave.

"Cade, wait!"

I run after him,
the warm sand
gripping my feet
with each step
as if it were trying to tell me
to go slowly,
carefully.

He turns.

"You gave me your word."

"I'm sorry.
I'm just . . .
I'm worried about you.
I want to help you."

"You can't help me!
No one can help.
Don't you get it?
There's nothing anyone can do.
Nothing!"

Then he's walking away again.

And I follow.

Because I know that feeling—
that goddamn,
son-of-a-bitch,
asshole of a feeling—
better than anyone.

Nine months ago

Dear Jeanie and Allen,

Okay, you want to hear from me?

Here you go.

I can't believe you are doing this to me. I can't believe you actually think this is what's best for me—to know you and to share my life with you.

You aren't my parents! My parents have raised me and loved me for the past fifteen years, the way you raised and loved your daughter, Charlotte.

I'm sorry she died. I'm sorry! But why am I being punished for that? Why is my whole family being punished?

If you care even a little bit about me, you will drop this. You will let it go—let me go, to live the life I want to live.

Please. I'm begging you.

Let me go.

And leave me alone.

Amber

unexpected

But he doesn't leave.

He walks down the beach.
I realize his shoes are by my bag,
so he can't just leave.

I want to help him.
But maybe helping is doing
what we've been doing all day.
Hanging out.
Having fun.
Forgetting everything,
except what's in the moment.

                    I kick myself.

I should have kissed him
or asked for the penny
or thought of a movie with sushi in it.
Anything besides asking that question.
Anything.

I stop and decide
to give him some time
to get over it.

                  Please let him get over it.

We're friends now.
How could I *not* ask?
I had to ask.
And hopefully he'll realize that.

As I head back to
where our stuff is,
I hear my name
floating on the breeze
in the distance.

I turn and see her
running toward me.
Madison.

three's a crowd

After hugs and hellos,
she loops her arm
in mine, and as we walk,
she tells me
about combing each
and every beach in Newport,
until she finally texted me
to get my location.

Her own treasure hunt.

        Although, what kind of treasure am I?

"You didn't have to come," I say.
"I'm fine."

"No, cat, you are not fine.
"You came to the beach *by yourself*!
That is not fine!
That is freaky!"

"Except, I'm not by myself.
Not anymore."

She doesn't get it.
I turn and point to Cade.

Her eyebrows creep up
along with the corners
of her mouth.
"So, what other secrets are you hiding?"

She pulls me down
on the sand
where we sit side by side,
passing questions and answers
back and forth like we're on
a TV game show.

We're so engrossed,
we don't notice him
until his shadow falls over us.

"Cade," I say,
"this is my best friend, Madison."

"Hey, cat," Madison says.
"Thanks for taking care of my girl."

"Cat?" he asks.
"It's actually Cade.
Rhymes with 'wade'?"

I laugh.
"No, see, instead of 'dawg'?
It's 'cat'—her thang."

He crosses his arms and
tries to give her a smile.
"Yeah, well, since you're here,
looks like my job is done."

Panic rises up in me
like a seagull taking flight.

Madison is quick
to come to my rescue.

"I'm not staying.
Just needed to make sure she's okay.
And she is, so I'm outta here."

"I have something I need to do," he says.
"Why don't you go eat?"
He looks at me.
"I'll meet up with you later."

There's a look in his eye
that tells me I shouldn't argue.
I want to.
But I don't. We exchange numbers,
and before he goes, I say,
"Heads, you call me.
Tails, you call me."

His eyes are
little pools of sadness.
"I can't promise."

Without thinking,
I reach out and hug him.
I squeeze tighter than he does.
Because I don't want him to go.

I kiss his cheek.
"Call me," I whisper.

And then I let him go.

sugar and spies

We get in Madison's Kia,
and before I can even
get the words out,
she's reading my mind
like a best friend should.

"We're following him, right?" she asks.

I reach into my bag.
Jelly beans for dinner.

"Right as raspberry."

I'm lucky

When we got the news
about the court's decision,
Madison was right there,
making me brownies,
trying to cheer me up.

People always say
chocolate makes
everything
better.

      I say friends make everything better.

Six months ago

Dear Amber,

We have stopped writing for the past three months, as you requested. But obviously, we couldn't, and didn't, drop the case. And we are terribly sorry you are upset. It hurts us, but we understand.

We realize you are a very smart young woman, but the fact of the matter is, you're still a child and we're sure you can't quite grasp the concept of what this all means, now or for the future.

Again, as we've said all along, we are family. It's only right that we know each other, rely on each other, and love each other.

We are thinking about you now that the verdict has come down from the judge. We are happy knowing that soon you'll come here to share your life with us. You have so many people here who are anxious to meet you—grandparents, aunts, uncles, and cousins! It's going to be wonderful, just wait and see.

Your parents have asked us to give you some time to come to terms with the court's decision. They seem to think this will be better for you in the long run. So we are granting them the first turn of shared custody. They will get their six months, and then we will get ours. We look forward to seeing you in March!

Much love,
Jeanie and Allen

extraordinary

"He's cute," Madison says
as she gnaws on what's left
of her thumbnail.

"I know.
He's cool, too.
He writes songs
and he loves movies—"

Then I stop because
I don't need to give
my best friend
a Cade commercial.

If I'm sold,
she's sold.

"How'd you meet?"

"We were both in awe of the jellyfish," I say.
Like it's the most ordinary way
to meet someone.

Nothing ordinary about it.
Nothing ordinary about this day.

Mostly, nothing ordinary about Cade.

Some friendly insight

He goes into
a fishing supply store.

We sit across the street.
Watching.
Waiting.

Madison throws
question after question at me,
and I shoot back
short answers,
too distracted to say
anything more.

I am focused
on the front door.

"Wow, this is bad," she says.

I whip around to look at her.
"What? What's bad?"

"You've fallen for him, cat."

"What?" I laugh.
"He's my friend.
I mean, we only met eight hours ago."

"I've known you a long time, A.
I've never seen you like this."

I turn back to the window.
Watching.
Waiting.
Wrestling

        with the idea that my best friend is
        right.

me and him

So, I care.

I care about his love of the beach.
I love it too.

I care about his songwriting.
I want to know more.

I care about the boy
who watched the sharks
and wished for confidence like that.
I understand.

I care about the fact
that's he's hurting,
even if I don't know why.
I want to help him.

That's why I'm here,
wanting to know what he's doing.

He's like me.
I want to know more.
I understand.
I want to help him.

And I care. A lot.

dark thoughts

Cade cradles
a black ball
in both hands
and carries it
to his car.

The way he walks,
the way he holds it,
I know it's heavy.

> Like a cannonball.

But Cade's not a pirate
so it can't be a cannonball.

Can it?

He carries one.
A staff person
follows with another.

Why?
Why are they carrying
heavy round weights
to his car?

Have you seen that movie?

Master and Commander?

Hollom grabs a cannonball
and jumps into the ocean.
He's so distraught,
he doesn't want to live anymore.

I know.

Oh my God, I know.

our day

Jellies and sea stars,
sharks and rays.

> A day of wonder,
> of magic, no fright.

Warm sun on skin,
sweet taffy on tongues.

> A day of exchanges,
> of finding delight.

Ghost in the lighthouse,
tunes in the car.

> A day of adventure,
> of seeking the light.

Castle on sand,
kite on a string.

A day of discovery,
of reaching new heights.

A day
that must not,
cannot,
end in any kind
of terrible
way.

Six months ago

Dear Mom,

Remember when I was like ten years old and I wrote you all kinds of notes after I learned about sex because I was too afraid to ask you the questions to your face?

Now I'm afraid to admit—I don't know how I'm going to be able to do this.

How do I leave everything I know, everything I love, everything I am, to go and live with them?

It's like a nightmare and I can't wake up. I don't know what to do. Please tell me, what do I do?

Love you,
Amber

caught

Madison and I
don't exchange words.

She knows I'm scared
as I eat my fill of
strawberry,
lemon,
popcorn, and
cotton candy
jelly beans.
She drives,
staying close
but keeping her distance,
so he won't notice
and try to lose us.

We follow him to the marina,
where fishing boats bob
to the smooth jazz
of the sea.

She grabs a parking spot
and I tell her to stay there,
sounding much stronger
than I feel.

He hauls one of the
lead weights onto a dock.
I follow him,
the smell of fish
rising up to greet me.

Before I know it,
he's stepped onto a boat.

                    Indecision grips me.

Do I go to him?
Do I hang back and watch?
He might be pissed
I followed him.
And yet
I don't want
the unthinkable
to happen either.

In the act of
weighing my options,
precious seconds tick by,
and I don't have to choose
because he chooses for me.

He's there,
off the boat
and back on the dock,
looking at me.

"Are you serious?"

"Cade, I was worried."

"I said I'd call you."
I flinch as the sharp
words come at me.

"I know, but—"

"Amber, I have to tell you,
I don't like stalkers.
I mean, this is not cool."

I swallow and nod.

"Stay here," he orders.

The sun is setting
in the distance.
I wish we were on
the beach,
watching,
playing,
laughing
like we were before.

I close my eyes and wish.
Please remember how we were before.

He comes back
carrying the other weight
he'd left in the car.

He takes a deep breath,
looks at the boat for a second,
then looks back at me.

This time,
his words are softer.
"All right.
 Follow me."

a good son

Black letters
on the hull say
THE GAL.

She looks much older
than the ones around her.
Smaller, too.

I step up and over,
onto the boat,
and watch as
Cade puts the lead weight
next to the other one,
near a big net.

"We lost a couple of these
last time we were out," he says.
"I was supposed to replace them
after our last trip."

"What are they for?"

"They keep the lines deep.
That's where the fish are."

Relief washes over me.

They're for fishing.
Not for drowning.

"Is this your dad's boat?"

"Yeah.
He's a commercial fisherman."

The wind has picked up,
and I wrap my arms
around myself, trying
to stay warm.

Cade doesn't seem to notice.
He's scanning the boat,
like he's lost something.
He steps past me,
and I want so much
to touch him,
to feel we're connected again.

But I wait,
because if drumming
has taught me anything,
it's that timing
is everything.

"Come on," he finally says.
"Let's go eat.
You must be starving."

But I don't move,
because there's something
more going on here.

"Can I meet your dad?"

He looks at me,
but the falling darkness
provides him
with a mask.

"No," he replies softly.
"Not today."

I guess that's
the only hint
I'm going to get.

together again

Back on the street,
Madison stands by her car,
the sun now tucked in tight,
the moon rising, ready
to take watch over our world.

I hug her and say good-bye.
No explanation necessary.
She knows this
is where I need to be.

Back in his Beetle,
a dozen questions
circle my mind like vultures.
I can't let them move in
on this moment though.

It's not time.
Now is the time
to let him know
he is safe with me.
That we can have fun
and be friends,
and it can be enough.

I'll make it be enough.

unnecessary

I get my words ready.
I want to tell him
I won't push him anymore.
That whatever's going on,
it's his business,
and whether he wants to tell me or not,
it doesn't matter, we can still
be friends.

Being a friend means
knowing when to push
and knowing when to pull back.

                    I'd forgotten that.

I get my words ready,
mixing them up and around,
wanting to say just
the right thing.

But while I'm
preparing,
sorting,
organizing,
stressing,
he speaks.

"I'll tell you, Amber.
I will tell you.
Just not now."

He reaches over for
my hand. Holds it there,
on my leg. My heart
skips a beat, and I give
his hand a little squeeze
as I put all of my
carefully selected words
away.

that's more like it

A pink lobster
glows neon
in the window.

Because it's dark,
I can't make out
the name of the place.

He leads me in,
waves at the guy
behind the register,
and takes me
to a booth in the corner.

It's obvious
he knows this place.
It's more than just somewhere
to get something to eat.

I look behind me
and see a bar
and pool tables.

We're underage,
but, obviously,
for reasons I don't understand,
it doesn't matter.

"So, no Chinese food?"

"Nope."
And that's all he says.

This boy likes to keep me guessing.

The waiter comes over,
says, "Hey, Cade,"
and asks if it'll be the usual.

"Yeah," he says.
"But two this time."

He knows what he wants.
No flipping coins.

I tell him I need to use the
restroom, so he gets up
and leads me to the back
where there are two doors,
one with a GONE FISHING sign
and one with a GONE SHOPPING sign.

"I hate shopping," I tell him.

"You can go in with me if you want."

Is he flirting with me?
Damn, I hope so.

piling it on

As I wash my hands,
I stare in the mirror,
thinking about this
weird and wonderful day.

It didn't turn out
like I thought it would.

                    Nothing ever does.

The good news is
I've hardly thought about
tomorrow at all.

The bad news is
I've now added new worries
to the pile that's so high,
it feels like it could topple over
at any moment.

Cade???
Why the hell are you here?
What can I do to help you?
Please, there must be something?
Will I ever see you again?
What if I don't like my new family?
What if my new family doesn't like me?
What if my real family doesn't miss me?
What if my real family even *likes* having me gone?

Wish I could demolish it
the way Cade destroyed
that sand castle.

If only it were that
easy.

hints of truth

My phone rings.

        It's my sister.

She yells at me,
says Mom and Dad
had a horrible day,
that I'm being selfish
and I should come home tonight
and not make them wait
until tomorrow.

I'm so tired of her yelling.
It's all she does lately,
going on about how
I'm not the only one
affected by the verdict.

But what the hell am I supposed to do?
I can barely keep it together myself;
how am I supposed to help her?
Help my parents?
Help my friends?

        I can't.

"Kelly, don't yell at me!
I needed to do this today.
I needed one day to myself.
Whatever I say, you're not going
to understand, but—"

"They think you're not coming back."
Her voice shakes as she says it.

"What? Why—"

"They think you don't want to go,
so you've run away.
And they feel bad, like they didn't
fight hard enough."

"I'm coming back."
But I say it like there's sand in my throat.

"You took your sticks."

"Yeah. So?"

"You took them, just in case.
Maybe you left, thinking you'd come back.
But admit it, Amber.
It's crossed your mind.
Not coming back."

I sigh as I run
my fingers through my
messy, sandy hair.

"Just come home. Please?"

"You're not gonna win this one, Kel.
I'm sorry.
Tell them I'm fine, all right?
And I'll see you tomorrow."

She sniffles.
"Love you, Jelly."

"Love you too, Kelly Belly.
I gotta go."

I hang up,
my heart racing,
the back of my neck sweaty.

"Hey, Amber?"
Cade knocks.
"You okay?"

"I'll be out in a minute."

Cade's words echo
in my head.

I bet others would say screw *it,*
and just not go back.

Six months ago

Dear Amber,

Like I told you when you were ten, you can tell me anything, ask me anything, even if you have to write it down.

Here's what you have to remember—you are a strong girl. I admire you and your strength. Look at how you helped your sister, and even me at times, through the divorce. You have such a good head on your shoulders.

You can do this. You can! And you know we'll be right by your side doing everything we can to help you through this.

Although you will have to leave the things and people you love, you'll always come back to them. You aren't losing us, sweetheart. I know it may feel that way, but you're <u>not</u> losing us! We can talk every day on the phone, we can do Skype chats, I'll even come down a couple of times and spend the weekend with you. I've already checked with Allen and Jeanie, and they said they wouldn't have any problem with that.

We must stick together and adjust to this big change.

Thank you for letting me know how you feel. I'm always here for you—don't ever forget that. No matter where you are, I'm here for you.

I love you,
Mom

more surprises

Back at the table,
I want to put everything
out of my mind
except for Cade.

While we wait for food to come,
we stick to safe
topics of conversation.

Our favorite seafood—
him: lobster
me: crab

What we like to read—
him: graphic novels
me: realistic fiction

Our pets—
him: a dog named Boo
me: a cat named Tiny

How said pets got their names—
him: white like a ghost
me: the fattest cat you've ever seen

How many girlfriends/boyfriends we've had—
him: two
me: one (although I don't tell him it was one
of those fake fifth-grade romances)

Whether we are attached at the moment—
him: no
me: no

And then we get
quiet.

Luckily the waiter
brings our food.
Steak and lobster.

"Uh, this is your usual?" I ask.

"My mom's a vegetarian.
I can't eat like this at home.
Plus, my older brother owns the place."

"Family discount, then?"

He smiles.

"Thanks.
For bringing me here."

As if on cue,
music starts to play.
It sounds like it's coming
from upstairs.
I take my knife and fork
and tap out the beat
on the table.

It makes him laugh.
"I had a feeling you might like it here."

And I have a feeling,
as the drumbeats
get louder,
that he is exactly right.

where I belong

Bellies full
of surf and turf
and spirits tired
of trying too hard
to keep things simple,
we head upstairs.

A small crowd
has gathered
to listen to the band.

The loud, fast music
with a hard edge
comes at us,
and I feel it

                    slicing
                    us

wide open.

They want us
to feel the loudness,
not just hear it.

And people do,
raising their fists
in the air,

punch,
        punch,
                punching it out,
showing the band
they're with them
all the way.

It's not the best
music in the world,
and who knows
what the hell
the lyrics are,
but right now,
loud works.

I watch the drummer
and focus on
the rhythm he plays.

He pounds out
the beats
with purpose,
and my arms ache
to make some noise.

Cade leans in,
yells in my ear,
"Do you want to play?"

"What? With them?" I ask.
"Yeah. I know them.

They're cool."

They finish the song and the
lead singer bends down
to grab his drink.

"But I don't know their songs."

"I bet you can find something."

I can't deny it. I'd love to play.
Still, I try to keep it cool.
"Sure. If they're up for it."

He runs up onstage and
I see him talking
and pointing at me.

It's not long before
I'm onstage, Cade
introducing me
to the band members,
Martin, Chase, and Henry.

"How about some White Stripes?" I ask.

"*Seven Nation Army*?" Henry suggests.

I nod.
Awesome.

The drummer, Chase,
jumps offstage and heads
for the bar.

I sit down.

I raise my arms in the air.

And before I know it,
there is nothing in this
world except me
and the rhythm
and the music
and the display of fists
telling me that right now,
everything is exactly
how it should be.

music is such an aphrodisiac

It's the release
I needed.

I play like a girl
possessed.

The boys offer me
the gift of
a solo, so I take it,
open it up,
and make it mine.

All mine.

When we're through,
the crowd yells
and I take a bow,
gratitude dripping
off of me.

I give my temporary
bandmates a wave
and jump down
into Cade's arms.

He spins me around
saying words like
"amazing" and
"incredible."

And I think to myself,

Yes you are,
yes you are,
yes you are,
yes you are,
yes you are.

take me there

Henry tells the
expanding crowd
the band is taking a break
and will be back in ten.

Cade disappears
for a minute,
then comes back
with a guitar.

When he takes the stage,
I can feel him taking
my soul
right along
with him.

He looks over at me.

"This one's for you."

"Blue sky,
sun on skin.
Open road,
take it in.

It's this feeling I get
that I can't seem to find
except when I let
all the worries unwind
when you're there by my side.
When you won't let me hide.

Let's go for a ride.

Hand in hand,
feelings sincere.
All we need
we'll find right here."

His voice, smooth as
water, washes over me.
And I am there,
on that road, the sun
warm on my skin,
and a feeling
of happy anticipation
fills me.

And when it's over,
tears fill my eyes
because it's not
the road that I'm on.

And I want it to be.

God, how I want it to be.

One month ago

Dear Amber,

We are starting to get things ready for your arrival.

*We're converting the guest room into your bedroom.
We'll provide the basics for now, and once you get
here, I'll take you shopping so you can decorate
any way you'd like.*

*Allen insisted you have a bookcase so you can fill it
with books. When we met you in the attorney's office,
you said you liked to read, and Allen remembered that.
If you have some specific titles you'd like him to get
for you, please drop him a note. He'd be more
than happy to have them waiting for you.*

*We're both getting so excited to have you here! Can't
believe, after all this time, you'll be joining us soon.*

*Is there anything you'd like me to know about food
preferences, allergies, etc. before you arrive? Otherwise,
we'll figure it all out when you get here.*

Love,
Jeanie and Allen

me and you

When Cade rejoins me,
he sees that I've gone
from elation to devastation
in the strum of a chord,
and I can tell it hurts him.

"It's not you," I tell him
as he pulls me into a corner.
"You were great.
You *are* great.
Too great, really."

He wipes away a tear
so gently
it's like an invitation
for more to fall.

But I close my eyes
and force them back
because he doesn't need that.

And then,
in the moment
of wishing away tears
and wanting to live
in his song,
his lips touch mine.

It's a soft kiss at first,
tender like he is,
and then stronger
as we pull
each other closer,
wanting to push
everything else away
except

        this.

the feeling's mutual

My emotions
are on a
bungee chord.
Plummeting
one minute and
rebounding the next.

When he pulls away,
he whispers, "Better?"

I smile.
"Much."

                    "Let's get out of here."

He takes my hand
and holds it
like he owns it.

And as we leave,
I realize for the
first time
in a long time
I'm not secretly scared
by someone wanting
to be with me,
but instead
so very grateful
for it.

so much goodness

Outside,
the night has
gotten colder,
but I embrace it
like an old friend.

It feels good.

Suddenly
everything
feels

good.

We walk to the
grocery store
on the corner.

"Did you see that movie?" I ask.
"Although, the book was better."

From his face,
I can tell
he has no clue.
It's not really obvious.
So I tell him.
"*Nick and Norah.*
The night in New York City?
It feels a little like that.
Except not as cool."

"Yeah," he says
as we head for the
school supply section.
"I'm not cool.
Not like you, drummer girl."

"You are too cool."
I pause. "Castle boy."

He laughs.

"Sounds like a bad boy band.
Introducing the Castle Boys!"

I grab
a small container
of glitter.

Because this day,
this wonderful,
beautiful,
glorious day,
just wouldn't be complete
without a little,
or a lot, of

g   i   t   r
  l   t   e

a dream come true

Our next stop
is a part of town
I'm not familiar with.

Cade parks on a street,
near the beach,
in front of a row
of small houses,
and while I admire
the hazy moon,
he gathers everything
we need from the
trunk of his car.

Apparently that
consists of a blanket,
a flashlight, a bottle of water,
and a hat, which he hands to me.

His concern for
my well-being
makes my heart
pound out a rockin' solo
inside my chest.

We walk down to the beach,
and he lays out the blanket
near a hole in the sand
that contains a log
with glowing embers.

I'm thinking about
me and him
and a fire
and a blanket.
And then I'm yelling,
"Wait!"
because maybe
I'm a tiny bit nervous
about me and him
and a fire
and a blanket.

He jumps back.

"Sorry.
I thought maybe we could
throw the glitter first."

"Okay, then.
Let's do it."

I take the bottle
of glitter and pour
some in my hand
and some in his.

"Should we do something first?" I ask.

"Yes. Close our mouths."

"No, I mean, make a wish or something?"

"Okay.
Out loud or to ourselves?"

"To ourselves."

So, quietly, we wish,
and when I think it's been
sufficient wishing time,
I say, "Ready. Set.
No—stop, it's too dark.
I have to get the flashlight."

I hold the flashlight
above my head and shine
it on him like a spotlight.
"You first, Cade.
Ready, set, go!"

His hand flies up
and sparkles rain down on him.
He spins around,
pretending to be a ballerina
dancing in the glitter,
and it makes me laugh.

"My turn."

He takes the flashlight
and places me in
the spotlight this time.
I toss the glitter
and hold my hands out,
trying to catch some
like a child tries to catch
snowflakes.

For a moment
the air is pretty,
sparkly,
and full of wonder.

But in a breath,
it's over.
He flicks off the light,
leaving us in darkness.

"Was it as thrilling as you thought?"

        "It was over too soon," I whisper.

He cups my face
with both hands,
leans in,
eyes lingering a
sweet second
before his lips
are there on mine,
teasing,
playing,
tasting,
kissing.

When he pulls away,
I'm breathless.

He nuzzles my ear.
"Now *that's* thrilling."

You got that right.

kissing

Lips on lips,
feel the heat.
Silky soft,
honey sweet.

Stay right here,
feed me more.
Lips on lips,
like never before.

wrap me up

I shiver.

He pulls away.
"Are you cold?" he asks.

"A little.
Plus . . . you know."

"What?"

"Um . . . your kisses?"

He laughs,
pulls me down
onto the blanket
and wraps his arms
and legs around me.

Perfect.
My kind of blanket.

burning bright

After a while
Cade tells me
he'll be right back.

I'm now
officially freezing,
so I wrap the blanket
around me.

He returns,
carrying twigs
and branches.

Bending down,
he blows on
the embers,
making them glow
brighter until
eventually
tiny flames dance.

I watch, amazed,
as he uses small twigs
at first, causing the flames
to reach higher and higher.
As the fire grows,
so does the size
of the firewood he uses.

I think back
to Passages of the Deep,
how we envied
the confidence
we saw there.

                    I feel it here.

Have we really changed
that much in twelve hours?

Cade sits down.
Kisses me again.
And I know we have.

don't you know?

"What'd you wish for, angel?" he asks.

Angel?
Is that my heart
f l u t t e r i n g
inside my chest?

"If I tell you, it won't come true."

"If you tell me, maybe I can make sure it does."

I look at him.
He makes me so
happy.
>Like playing my
>favorite songs
>in front of a
>million people
>>happy.

So I tell him.

>"I wished I could stay here with you."

smoke and mirrors

He doesn't answer.

The fire crackles and pops,
filling in the silence.

Smoke blows toward us.

"Smoke follows beauty," he says.

"Well, that wouldn't be me.
You and your song, though.
That's beautiful."

"You liked it?"

I kiss him.
"Yeah. I liked it."

"Amber?"

Oh, God.
The way he says it.
It's like bad news is coming.
Don't say it.
Don't tell me I can't stay.

Don't be like them,
thinking you know
what's best for me.
Please.
Don't be like them.

"What?"

"You *are* beautiful."

let chance decide

The fire
and Cade's arms
keep me warm.

I love the warmth.

"Think your family is worried?" he asks.
"It's getting late."

"I was supposed to stay at a hotel."

"Change of plans?" he asks,
trying to sound casual when
we both know it's not
a casual question at all.

"You could say that."

"Good. I want you here."

Silence settles around us.

But then I push it away,
wanting him to know
there's more to my wish
than what I told him.

"Cade, I don't want to go.
I mean, at all.
Heads, I stay.
Tails, I go?"

I surrender

It's true.
My wish for
one day
has turned into
a wish
for many days

        like this one.

For months
my life has been
one giant game
of tug-of-war.
I'm tired of the
pulling.
I need to let go,
to breathe, to remember
what life is about.
And it's about days

        like this one.

Is it really so wrong
to want to start over,
to build a life
where every day
I wake up
and have a beautiful day

       like this one?

Two weeks ago

Dear Amber,

I made a reservation for us at the beach.
For the night before you leave.
We can spend a lovely day there,
stay at the hotel, get up early, and come
home, filled with wonderful memories.

How's that sound?

Love,
Mom

Two weeks ago

Dear Mom,

Please don't be mad. Please?

I love that you want to take me to my favorite place on earth. I love how you knew it would comfort me at a time when not much else could.

But I think I want to go to the beach by myself. Would that be all right? It's nothing personal. You know I love you guys. I'd just like some time by myself before I go. I can't explain why I need to do this. I just do.

Thanks for making the reservations. You're so good at knowing what I need.

You're so good at being my mom!

Love,
Amber

taking control

"You have to remember, Amber.
Staying would mean losing
the good along with the bad."
He looks at me.
"You'd lose everything."

I stroke his cheek.
"Not everything."

"It's really not something you
should leave to chance."

Maybe not.
Maybe I don't flip a coin.
Maybe I simply make the choice.

Tear my life
from their hands
and put it back where
it belongs—into my own.

It would be so much easier
if I wasn't two long
years away from eighteen.

It's such an impossible situation.

Cade takes my hand
and pulls me to
my feet.

"Are we leaving?" I ask.

"I want to show you something," he says.

going, going—where?

We leave everything
behind on the beach.

The blanket,
the fire,
the glitter,
my bag.

It's all there,
so we'll be back.

More than that,
we aren't going far.

the reveal

Up the beach,
through a gate,
around a greenhouse,
through a sliding-glass door,
and into a home.

A stale smell
greets us,
and I have to resist
the desire to run
to a window
and throw it wide open.

Cade flips the light switch
and we're standing
in a kitchen where
faded wallpaper
of old, country
kitchen utensils
clings to the walls.

Dirty dishes stacked
on every available surface
cry out for attention.

I can almost taste the despair.

He leads me
to another room
and turns on the light.
It's a family room
and everywhere I look—
on tables, on top of
the entertainment center,
on the walls—
there are family photos.

I walk over to
a framed collage
with pictures of two boys and
a young man who I assume
is his dad because he looks
just like Cade.

Photos of them
on the boat,
at the aquarium,
at the beach,

           digging holes,
           building sand castles,
           flying kites.

I whisper, afraid of waking someone.
"Your dad lives here?"

"You don't have to whisper.
They're not home."

"Where are they?"

"At the hospital."

With just a few words,
so many questions
answered.

That's why he was alone
today.

That's why he said no more pictures
today.

That's why he needed me
as much as I needed him
today.

his story

On an old floral couch
that smells nothing
like flowers and
everything like cigarettes,
he tells me what he's
been keeping close
to his heart.

The words come out
slowly, like they've
been forced inside
for so long,
they're hesitant
to come out.

Cade's dad has cirrhosis,
or liver disease,
and he desperately needs
a transplant.

He and Cade's stepmom, Marian,
are at a hospital
in Portland, with
a transplant
scheduled for
tomorrow morning.

"Isn't that good news?" I ask.

And then,
more words,
even slower
than before.

"Amber,

I

am

the

donor."

dangerous

I think back to
our safe
conversations,
and it was like
watching the sharks
and the rays
behind the thick glass.

It's where
we needed
to be.

But now we're done watching.
We've jumped in.

        We're swimming with the sharks.

me: Why aren't you in the hospital?
him: Don't have to be. I'm healthy. I just report for surgery
tomorrow.

me: How long has your dad been there?
him: A while. They've been monitoring him. Marian's staying
with a friend in Portland.

me: Don't you have tests to do? Something?
him: Already did them earlier in the week.

me: It's major surgery, Cade! What are the rules?
him: Take it easy. No aspirin for three days prior. No food or drink after midnight.

me: Shouldn't you be resting, then?

He scoots close to me.
His hand reaches out
and tucks a piece of my hair
behind my ear.
His eyes reach out to me,
trying to reassure me.
Or maybe himself.

him: I'm pretty sure being with you is the most restful place I can be.

taking chances

Without my asking,
he tells me more.

They'll take a piece
of Cade's liver
and give it to his dad.

The piece will survive.
Grow.
Thrive.
Or so they hope.

His dad will survive.
Grow stronger.
Get better.
Thrive.
Or so they hope.

Cade will be hospitalized
for a week, maybe longer,
with many weeks of recovery
at home after that.

He will survive.
Get better.
Thrive.
Or so they hope.

Chances are small
that anything will go
wrong.

But that's where the problem lies.

There is still that chance.

Heads: It goes well.
Tails: It doesn't.

go away

I think of fear,
like the boogeyman.

He's the guy with no face
who hides in every
dark place you know of
and especially those you don't.

As much as you
tell yourself he
can't get you,
that angels
watch over
and protect you,
he is there,
in those
dark places,
waiting.

I know the boogeyman.
He's tormented me
for years.

Cade knows him too.

I see him hiding
in Cade's breath
and Cade's words.

And there is nothing
I want more
right now
than to chase him

away.

the truth hurts

Pain hides
behind his
beautiful
brown eyes.

"I want him to live," he says.

I watch,
helpless,
as the pain
slips out.

T
e
a
r
s

f
a
l
l

when he whispers,

"But damn it, I want to live too."

what if

And now I see
that all day,
he's been thinking
about his options.

At first it feels
like all you can do
is what you're
told to do.

But then other options
start to appear.

They creep in,
tap you on the shoulder,
whisper your name.

Because there are *always* options.

They might not be popular.
But there they are.

They start to look good.
Better and better
as time goes on.

And the way that makes you feel?
Yeah, it gives you the hope
you've been searching for.

And pretty soon,
you're looking around,
wondering,

What if?

One week ago

Dear Jeanie and Allen,

*You can't make me go. You can't! If I refuse to go,
what are you going to do? Have me arrested?
This whole thing is ridiculous.*

You don't want me.

*You want Charlotte back! I don't care what
you say. If you had your other daughter, you wouldn't
want me. But you can't have her, so you're going to
take me instead.*

It's bullshit! The whole thing is BULLSHIT!

Amber

a familiar place

Pretty soon
Cade takes my hand
and leads me
back to the beach.

We sit in front of the fire.
I rub his back
and try to think of something
helpful I can say.

The fire dwindles.
Silence settles around us
once again.

I know he's remembering.
He's thinking of
all those times
they built sand castles,
flew kites,
caught fish—
holding on to them
like they're the
last memories on earth.

And he's wishing.

He's wishing hard
that they're not.

a discovery

"Cade?"

He looks at me.
Ribbons of tears
stream down his face.

I brush them away
with my thumb
and smile,
trying to keep
my own from falling.

                    "It will be okay."

"But—"

"Do you know how difficult
it must have been for your dad
to ask you to do this for him?
He wouldn't have asked if he
didn't think you'd be okay."

Cade quickly wipes his face
with the back of his hand.
"That's what the doctors say.
But, Jesus, they're cutting me open.
Taking a part of my body.
There's the chance of blood clots,
of infection, and a hundred other things."

"But if you don't do it . . ."

I stop.
I let his thoughts rest there for a second.
He knows. Of course he knows.

But throughout the day
he's been trying to tell himself
maybe there's a chance for the
heavens to open up and a
miracle will rescue them all.

I've been the same way.

If I just ignore it,
pretend it isn't happening,
get some distance,
maybe somehow,
some way,
everything will magically

                              change.

And suddenly I get it.

There isn't magic out there.
There is magic *here*.

Right here, in this place
that brought us together
the day before
we face our fears
and our lives change forever.

Magic in the jellies.
Magic in the lighthouse.
Magic in the music.
Magic in the kisses.
Magic in the glitter.

Magic in us.

What we need
will appear
right when we need it.

Just like it did
today.

alike more than different

I snuggle in close
and kiss him.
He tastes like
campfire and
salty air.

"I'm sorry," I tell him.
"My stuff must seem so trivial to you."

"No. Not at all."

> "But it's not a matter of life and
> death."

"To your new parents, I think it is.
Losing you would be like
another daughter dying."

"But how can you lose something you've never had?"

"You're their daughter," he tells me.
"You're connected, whether you like it or not."

"Do you ever wish it were someone else?" I ask.
"Like, your brother instead?
I've wished it were my sister.
Which is just so wrong.
Why would I wish this on anyone?"

He kisses me.
"Because you're human."
He sighs.
"Just like me."

imagine

And because we are human,
we feel it all—
the anger,
the sadness,
the fear,
the resentment.

Regardless
of how many people
tell us
everything will be fine,
             we'll live,
                  life will go on—
we can't help
but feel
it all.

In the park
one day on a walk,
my dad told me
that my feelings
wouldn't last
forever.

He said one day,
though it's hard to imagine,
they'd be replaced
by new ones.

Good or bad,
they would be replaced.

I think about that
and see my dad is probably
right.

When Cade's surgery
is over and he's fine,
and his dad is getting better,
all these bad feelings
he has now
will be replaced—
by gratitude and love.

I wish he could just

skip forward.

And so I say,
"Cade, close your eyes."

"What?"

"Just do it. Close them."
I wait. He does.

"Imagine four weeks from today,
you're at home, watching movies,
ripping through Netflix.
Your friends come by,
bring you some dirty magazines,
or some graphic novels,
and they're like, Hey Cade,
you look good, how's your dad?
And you break out this gigantic smile
because you can tell them
He's doing good.
Better than good.
He's at home, getting better,
calling me every day,
bugging the crap out of me."

I look at him.
It's all over his face.
Gratitude and love.

I lean in and whisper,
"Keep your mind *there*."

an agreement of sorts

In my family
my dad was always
the brave one.

The one who'd
check under
my bed and in
my closet
at bedtime
to make sure
the monsters were gone.

The one who'd
kill the giant spider
while Mom, Kelly, and I
went screaming
into the other room.

The one who'd
sleep with a baseball bat
under his side of the bed,
ready for intruders.

I reach for the
silver sand dollar
hanging from my neck,
hidden under my shirt.
I missed Dad when he moved out.
I still miss him sometimes,
even though we see each other often.
I miss seeing him at the dinner table
or on the couch watching a game.
I just miss him being there.

I try to imagine
myself in Cade's shoes,
having to be the brave one
for a change.

Having to rescue my dad
from the big, ugly spider.

I'd be scared, but I'd do it.
Just like I know
Cade is going to do it.

He reaches over
and touches my
silver dollar.

"It's beautiful," he says.

"A gift from my dad."

He nods.
Waits a minute.
"My dad didn't ask me to do it, you know.
To be the donor.
I volunteered.
I just . . . I didn't know I'd be this scared."

Now *that* is a beautiful gift.

"I think the fear is normal, Cade.
Just don't let it win."

He whispers, "I won't if you won't."

sweet dreams

It's cold.
And late.
We pack up
and head inside.

Cade has to be at
the hospital by eight.

"You need sleep," I tell him.
"Let's rest for a few hours."

In a chilly, dark room
at the back of the house,
we crawl into his bed,
and we spoon.

I've been wondering something.
So I ask him.
"What was with the boat today?"

He strokes my hair.
Kisses my ear.

"I want to tell Dad it's ready to go.
That it's here, waiting for us.
That in four or five months, we'll be fishing again."

I smile.
That's good.

Fear isn't the only thing he's feeling.

"Did you see that movie?" I ask after a while.

He mumbles, "What?"

He's so tired. Almost asleep.

"*Hope Floats*," I whisper.
"I've always loved that title."

messy

I can't sleep.
My thoughts won't let me.

So, while he sleeps,
I go to the kitchen,
and I clean.

All those dirty dishes,
left behind by a woman
consumed with worry.
She shouldn't have to
come home to them
and be reminded
of that worry.

She should come home
and feel relieved.
Relieved the worst is over.
Relieved the house is clean.

The act of scrubbing
soothes my soul, just a little.

Still, my thoughts
keep spinning
around and around
like the sponge
in my hand.

How can I leave him?

How can I say good-bye,
let him go to the hospital,
a place he hates,
a place he fears?

I put the last dish away.
The kitchen is clean.

But everything else?
What a mess.

crunch time

I open the sliding-glass door
to let the cool breeze
rush in and chase away
the stale air.

Goose bumps rise
on my arms.

The waves pound the shore
in the distance, and home
seems so far away.

I think of Mom in bed,
trying to sleep,
but thinking of me.
Maybe Kelly's with her.
I hope she's with her.
The affectionate one.
The pretty one.
The one who looks like Mom,
with her blue eyes and blond hair.

Kelly was right.
I was selfish,
to do this to them.

But I had to come.
I had to get away.
The day before
your life changes
is a big day.

But it's not
the day before
anymore.

            The day is here.

The day I've dreaded,
and now dread even more,

is here.

Three days ago

Dear Amber,

I know we've been fighting a lot lately.

I know you think I hate you more than I love you.

I know it might seem like I don't care that all of this is happening to you.

So I just wanted to tell you, I do care. And believe it or not, I'm going to miss you.

Remember—you will be back.

We'll be waiting.

I love you, Jelly.
Kelly Belly

stronger than I thought

At five I wake
Cade with kisses
and cuddles.

"Can't we just stay here?" he whispers,
holding me so tight,
there is nothing else
in the entire world
but me and him.

My heart
begs me to say
yes.

But my brain tells me
regret would come,
knocking loudly,
invading this sweet space
and ruining everything.

       I wish time would stop.

But whether on sea stars
or under glitter
or in Cade's arms,
wishes don't always come true.

So I kiss him
one more time
and apologize
to my very
fragile heart.

"Time to go, baby."

hearts in the sand

He leads me
to the beach
one last time.

I understand.
It feels wrong to leave
without wishing the ocean
a proper good-bye.

It's still dark, but
the moon glows,
smiling down on us.
Cade grabs a stick.
Makes a big heart in the sand.
Writes AMBER.

I take the stick.
Intertwine a heart with his.
And I write CADE.

Then he wraps
his arms around me,
our bodies intertwined
like the hearts and
our connection so strong,
it's impossible
we only met yesterday.

It's not long enough.

Damn it.
It's just not long enough.

here we go

"Let me take you home?" he asks.
"On my way to Portland?"

I smile.
"I wouldn't have it any other way."

the road back

He drives.

I call the limo driver
and cancel my ride.

He drives.

I text my mom and dad
and tell them I'll see them soon.

He drives.

I lean in and kiss his cheek.
Turn up the song,
Falling In by Lifehouse.

He drives.

The sun rises.
The sky lights up
with all the pretty sky colors,
just like yesterday.

I turn to Cade.
"You are my sky."

And I want to feel happy,
but the closer we get,
the sadder I feel.

He still drives.

I grip his leg.
Squeeze it tight.

"Slow down," I say.

But of course he can't.
He has an appointment.

So he drives.
And I start to cry.

I want the happy ending

Cade pulls over.

"I don't want to go," I say.

"I know. Me neither."

"Let me go with you.
I can take care of you.
I'll be the best nurse ever."

He takes my face
in his hands and
looks at me with
those gorgeous brown eyes
that I lose myself in
like the sweetest of songs.

"Did you see that movie?"

I think.
I think hard.
Boy leaving?
Girl crying?
What is it?
But I'm too sad
and I'm drawing a blank.
I shake my head.

"Lloyd Dobler ring any bells?"

Another of my mom's favorites.
Say Anything with John Cusack.

He goes on.
"That scene, where Lloyd holds
the radio above his head?
Think of me. Every night, think of me,
and pretend I'm doing that."

I shake my head.
"But he goes with her.
They end up together.
It's not fair."

He kisses me.

"Who says we don't end up together too?"

getting closer

I reach for my bag.
Get out my jelly beans.
But I eat alone,
because he's having surgery
and can't eat anything.

Oh my God.
The steak and lobster was like his last meal.
Of course he wanted something good.
Something great.
Because what if—

I shake my head.
Pop in another jelly bean,
cream soda this time,
and Cade looks at me funny.

"They help me.
I know, it's weird.
They just do."

"What's your least favorite flavor?" he asks.

"Licorice. Yours?"

"Buttered popcorn."

"And your favorite?" I ask.

"Sour cherry."

"You should write a song.
A song about jelly beans.
That'd be cool."

He smiles.
"Maybe I will.
I'll call it *Amber and Her Jellies*."

"And they'll think,
Amber's eating jellyfish?"

We laugh.

My mind drifts back
to that first moment
when I saw him,
admiring their loveliness,
while I admired him.
His beautiful face.
His intense stare.
His skinny jeans.

And I guess he goes back too.
"In case you don't know," he says,
"I'm really glad we met."

I squeeze his leg again.
"Holy shit, Cade,
I don't even know your last name."

"Cummings. Caden Cummings.
No relation to the poet."

"Amber Jacobson.
But you already know that.
And no relation to the golfer."

"We'll have to exchange e-mails.
Addresses. Everything."

"It's all yours," I tell him.

And I mean it.
He can have it all.
He's already got the most
important thing anyway.

My heart.

and closer

"I'll see you again," he asks.
"Right, angel?"

When he calls me that,
I get all tingly.

Though I can tell,
it's less about me
and more about him.
Eight o'clock is getting closer
by the minute.

"Yes, Cade.
I promise.
You'll see me again."

By the way? You're my angel too.

One day ago

Dear Mom,

I wish I was as strong as you think I am. You keep telling me I can do this, and I just keep thinking, No I can't! I honestly don't know how I'm going to get through these next six months. Grandma said she'd send a guardian angel to Texas. I'm like, can you send an army of them?

I know you and Dad love me and support me. I know you'll do everything you can in the coming months to make my life better. But I still have to be the one to go.

Anyway, I'm sorry I want this day to myself. I know you're probably sad about that. Hopefully, you understand.

And I'll be back. Because I love you.

Please don't worry. See you tomorrow.

Love,
Amber

thank you, God

We're almost to my house.
I want to tell him
to keep driving.
To get on the freeway
and take me with him.

I want to tell him
I'm too scared to go
and I really
can't do this.

That I talk a good talk
and I tell other people
it will be okay,
but when it comes to me
and my world being
ripped apart,
I can't do it.

Out of nowhere Cade asks,
"Do you think about her?"

"Who?"

"The other girl.
The girl who died."

"Sometimes."

"If you hadn't been,
you know, switched,
your parents would be
the sad ones."

"Yeah."

"Crazy how an accident
worked out for the best, huh?
Like us running in to each other.
I mean, what are the chances?
Makes me think maybe God
does know what He's doing."

Does He?
Or is it all chance?

Heads: This girl.
Tails: That girl.

Me
or
her.

And that's when it hits me
like a stick on the toms.

         I'm the lucky one.

that's what it is

Life is the bad
with all the good.

The deadly sharks
with the beautiful sea stars.

The gigantic waves
with the sand castles.

The licorice
with the lemon and lime.

The loud lyrics
with the rhythm of the music.

The liver disease
with the love of a father and son.

It's life.

Sweet, beautiful,
wind on your face,
air in your lungs,
kisses on your lips
life.

is that a promise?

I point the way.

And even though
I know it's coming,
and have been mentally
preparing myself,
when he stops the car,
I can't hold it in.

More tears fall.

Because I want him to be okay
and I want me to be okay,
but mostly I don't want him
to forget me.

He holds me,
kisses my tears,
and before I can speak,
he whispers,
"Let's set a place, to meet,
as soon as you're back.
Do you like the zoo?"

"Love it."

"Okay, the Oregon Zoo.
September twentieth, ten a.m."

And before I know it,
it's happening again.

"Did you see that movie?" I ask.

He pauses for a second.
He loves this part,
where I search his eyes,
wondering if he knows.

Then he smiles.
"*Before Sunrise*?
The most romantic movie ever,
according to my mom.
Yeah. Well,
I'll be there.
And so will you."

And oh my God, I believe him.
I really believe him.

parting is just plain sorrow

We exchange everything.
I tell him to call me
as soon as he can
and let me know
all is well.

"When do you leave?" he asks.

"My flight is at noon."

"Hopefully you'll sleep."

"Yeah," I say, poking him in the side,
"hopefully you will too."

And then laughter,
helping to fight back the tears.

He kisses me, softly,
like that first time.

"I wish I could be with you," I tell him.
And the laughter loses
as the tears fall again.

He can only nod.

I get my bag and open it.
I hand him my drumsticks.
"Keep them safe for me, okay?"

"You got it.
But I don't have anything for you."

I'm about to say it's fine,
when he holds his finger in the air
and reaches into his pocket.

He hands me the penny.
Our penny.
"To remember our lucky day," he says.

"I'll never forget," I whisper.

"Me neither."

There is one last kiss.
The longest one yet.

And then he's gone.

he's a good example

It's like
the silence
that follows

       the beautiful song.

Or
the darkness
that follows

       the glitter in the air.

He knew
what to do
to make it better.

As I walk toward
the door,
I take a deep breath.

I know
what to do
to make it better.

As he
embraced me,
I will
try to embrace
this day
that follows

the day before.

Two weeks later

Dear Cade,

A real letter this time. Decided to switch it up from our twenty e-mails a day. Besides, I wanted to send you a little something.

I'm so glad you are feeling better. Hope your mom is being nice to you—is she trying to serve you macaroni and cheese, the ultimate comfort food? Tell her you want clam chowder instead. With freshly baked bread.

In the morning, we're getting up early. Going to San Antonio for the weekend. Allen and Jeanie want to show me the Alamo. They're trying to talk me into getting some cowboy boots. Be careful. You may not recognize me when you see me in September.

Enjoy your box of jellies. It's open because I took out all the buttered popcorn ones, so you have nothing to worry about. I gave them to Allen. What do you know, he says he loves that kind. I wonder if that means you two wouldn't get along? Just kidding. I think they'd like you. And you would probably like them. They're all right.

Speaking of jellies, you should start working on my song.
Who cares if it hurts to sing, I want my song! (Actually,
I really hope you're not in too much pain. Have your
friends brought you any dirty magazines? I can ask
Allen to buy some and I'll send them to you—ha!)

Wish I could bring you presents in person. I think about
you all the time. In fact, I watched a good movie last
night, and wondered if you've seen it.

Guess which one.

Go on. Guess.

Hugs and kisses,
Amber